Fire in the Field
and Other Stories

In Praise of This Collection

I really did enjoy, no, *love* John Young's stories; they are a worthy heir to those of John Cheever and John Updike.

Young writes with an exceptional clarity and deep sympathy for his characters. The emotional range is very large, including real tragedy, humor, epiphanies large and small. Underneath them all remains the experiences of a white man of rural background, a mostly forgotten kind of narrator/hero/protagonist in today's politically charged world. The values of this rural Midwestern America continue to focus on the importance of high school sports in particular: fathers who played football expecting their dreams of ... glory to be reincarnated through their sons; mothers who push these sons relentlessly; "popular" girls who are the iconic cheerleaders, and the boys themselves, whose personalities vary more widely than our own high school memories would allow for.... It's a very masculine culture, old school style, and therein is one of Young's greatest strengths: he neither idealizes nor romanticizes those rural Midwestern towns that most of us now see as Trump country, fairly or not.

–Daniel Brown, Editor, *Aeqai* (*www.aeqai.com*)

John Young follows his fine first novel, *When the Coin Is In the Air*, with a book of stories of middle Americans faced with decisions – moral, ethical, romantic, financial – "while the coin is in the air."

–Dan Wakefield, author of *New York in the Fifties* and
How Do We Know When Its God?

I said *Let me read a few minutes of these stories before I start dinner.* At midnight I was still crying, laughing, and fond of Young's ability to take me with him. I entered a furniture repair shop rife with lies, the innards of a rotting pumpkin, a chainsaw-accident scene, 12 acres of burning hay.

At last, a father-son story that abandons schmaltz and tackles hilarity; bored-couple syndrome without melodrama; dialog so real I forgot I was in my living room.

That's my old minister, I thought, my neighbor, my sister-in-law, ME! Young focuses his people-reading and peers right through me, directing his spotlight onto my pride, mistakes and miseries.

Phrases such as "slowly cooking in the heat of anger..." and "lifting a layer of snow like a sheet on a clothesline," add as much impact as his uncanny understanding of who we are.

–Connie Shakalis, Columnist, *The Bloomington Herald-Times* (*ConnieShakalis.com*)

There's so much to like in this "album." The stories are well plotted and engrossing, the characters interesting, and the writing stunning. Young has unusual skill with language, an ear for voices, and a way with images. I like the shifts in perspective, the way protagonists struggle with the ethical implications of their actions, the themes of competition and sexual jealousy, and the way some seem satisfied with their positions in life (the joy of being a mailman) while their partners are restless, wanting something they think has higher status. Keeping the tone of the whole, each story provides a surprising shift in the nature of the dilemmas it addresses. My current favorite, the closing story, "In a Delicate Condition," is simultaneously heartbreaking and heartwarming.

–Joanna Marshall, Retired Professor of English Literature, University of Puerto Rico

As one story progresses to the next, Young's deceptively simple voice evolves; the innocent peculiarities become more complex, and the stories deepen shockingly – as if fate has caught us, and Young himself, in the best hopes of literature. *Fire in the Field and Other Stories* is the real thing.

–Frederick Dillen, author of the novels, *Hero, Fool*, and *Beauty*

What sets these exquisitely crafted stories apart is John Young's keen sense of place and his ability to make you feel you are there. Not just physical places, but states of mind too. And so you feel conflicted sitting with an anxious teenager talking with her mother. You are afraid alongside a boy chasing an angry father. You are bereft as you gaze upon the empty chair of the only friend who really understood you. In these 16 superb stories, you won't just read about such situations. You'll be immersed in them. You'll be transported.

–Don Tassone, author of *Francesca*

Fire in the Field and Other Stories by John Young is an elegant, wry, wise, witty collection that deserves a place among the best work being produced today. These are quintessentially middle-American stories with richly textured characters struggling to navigate the complex, morally compromised world in which they live. Young is a writer who knows his craft and deserves the attention of a wide audience.

–Patricia Averbach, author of *Resurrecting Rain*

I found Young's tales surprisingly satisfactory. People with small lives have large epiphanies; things shift. Each story is a micro-novel, a delicious no–cal snack that transports you to a place and time where you root ardently for new friend(s).

The stories are filled with ordinary people facing complex moral, ethical, romantic or financial decisions: a neophyte high school journalist whose mother doesn't see talent in him; a wife who must decide whether to try for a baby with her terminally-ill husband; an angry boy seeking revenge.... [Fire in the Field] is hard to put down. Memories flood back when you read these exquisitely–crafted tales: of mistakes one made that couldn't be undone; of crushes that almost became romances; of knotty family dynamics.

–Cynthia Smith, Journalist and reviewer, *Wyoming Living*

A Gift from John Updike to a Young Writer

When our author was a young writer living in Beverly, Massachusetts, he got to know John Updike. When "The Antique Deal," was published in Yankee in 1998, the famous writer sent this note. (Below the signature, Updike doodled two possible pronunciations for "patina.")

Congratulations; it's a lovely story, full of fine furniture details. It made me think I should change professions, but I'll have to learn how to pronounce 'patina.' Appearing in *Yankee* is a fine honor, even if some of the editing drew blood. It's a bloody business, in a way.

Best wishes,
John Updike

Fire in the Field
and Other Stories

by

John Young

To Antoni & Brigitth,

Thank you for being soup kitchen guilds first and deeper friends after.

All the best to you both,

Golden Antelope Press
715 E. McPherson
Kirksville, Missouri 63501
2021

ISBN   978-1-952232-56-5

Library of Congress Control Number: 2021935808

Published by:
Golden Antelope Press
715 E. McPherson
Kirksville, Missouri 63501

Available at:
Golden Antelope Press
715 E. McPherson
Kirksville, Missouri, 63501
Phone: (660) 665-0273
http://www.goldenantelope.com
Email: ndelmoni@gmail.com

For Lauren

Acknowledgements

One winter night, a writer friend of mine compared a short story collection to a record album–from the days of vinyl and CDs–where the first song sets the tone for the album and it ends with a strong one that makes you want to revisit the whole. Songs in the middle take risks and stretch for something new, different, and emotional. That made sense to me. Like those albums, your favorite story may be waiting in the middle of this collection. My hope is, like a favorite album, you'll revisit these stories and discover a new favorite each time.

*

There are so many people to thank for lending a hand in my life and on these stories. A consistent source of encouragement, learning, and support in my life is the creative cadre of Jeff Bell, Paul Kroner, and Ron MacLean. I also want to thank Neal and Betsy Delmonico at Golden Antelope Press. Their wit, intelligence, and encouragement kept me going. This is my second book with them, after my novel *When The Coin Is In The Air*. Two of the stories, "Fire in the Field" and "Enter Debbie DeVore" were chapters in the novel and appear here in a slightly edited form. Special thanks to Jeff Bell for pointing out those stories hiding in the novel. The story "A Pumpkin Summer" inspired my yet-to-be-published second novel: *Getting Huge*. "The Antique Deal" first appeared in *Yankee Magazine*.

I want to thank my former professors and classmates in the MFA program at Emerson College in Boston where a few of these stories began. Two writer friends offered insights and suggestions–thank you Don Tassone and Andrea Kay. Because books are judged by their covers, I owe a special debt to the graphic designer/illustrator who captured the spirit of these stories–thank you to my son, Nick Young.

As usual there's a family behind the artist, and in this, I am more fortunate than I deserve. To Lauren, my wife and north star, thank you for believing in me and encouraging me all these years. To my kids, Nick and Tess, it has been a great joy to see you grow into adults I admire and learn from. Thank you for your support on this book. And finally, to you, dear reader, thank you. I appreciate every reader.

Contents

The Antique Deal   3

A Pumpkin Summer   14

A Membrook Man   30

This Boy's Game   56

Twice Too Young   68

An Imperfect Union   73

The Dog Lover   95

Enter Debbie DeVore   106

The Chain Saw Artist   112

Same as I Got   124

The Fires of Youth   130

Wins and Losses   140

The Thing She Saw   147

Finding the Words   151

Fire in the Field   168

In a Delicate Condition   175

Fire in the Field and Other Stories

The Antique Deal

No one came to Carl Packer for good antiques. Collectors of Americana sought out Steven Hale or Rachel Goodson. Carl's shop operated under the grocery store approach: make a small margin and move the stock fast. He'd always wanted to be a high-end dealer, but Carl shrank from risking six thousand dollars for a cherry cupboard. What if it only brought three? It took truckloads of candlesticks, old glass bottles, and picture frames to cover a three-thousand–dollar blunder.

The last time Carl took such a risk—with that tiger maple dresser—it sat in his shop for months until he finally sold it to Rachel. She and Steven could turn a handsome profit from such a piece because they held the wish lists of wealthy collectors from all over the country, collectors who flew up to New Hampshire to see a piece, bought from smartphone snapshots, or sent their decorators. And the region's pickers–the tireless bloodhounds of the business who went door to door and shamelessly tailed old ladies home from church, asking if they had anything for sale, anything in the attic, the basement, the garage, the barn, the shed–these pickers took their booty to Steven and Rachel first. To find his merchandise, Carl spent weekends scouring yard sales, his hands powdered with the dust and mildew of attics and basements, hiring his daughter Shelly to watch the shop. And he idled through evening auctions, missing Shelly's choir programs, hoping against experience to skim treasures from box-lots at the end of sales.

The elite dealers of Early American antiques owned spectacular homes and small, tidy shops of two or three rooms, some open by appointment only. Until Edie divorced him five years ago, the Packers lived above his musty shop. Now Carl lived there alone.

Still, Carl was proud of his reputation as a knowledgeable and honest dealer, one who was quick to point out a repair on a piece of pottery or a pie safe. But after selling Steven Hale or Rachel Goodson a fine antique, he imagined them saying, "Good guy, honest as the day is long. What a chump."

One April night Carl Packer lay in bed. Mortgage, taxes, and insurance had dogged his entire adult life, but what vexed him now was Shelly's plan to attend the University of New Hampshire. To atone for the divorce, Carl had promised to pay for a state college: tuition, room and board, books–the whole shebang. In five months his girl would pack off to UNH. Or not. Although he'd boasted to Shelly of a college fund, he hadn't saved a dime.

The next morning, Carl shook off his weariness and pledged to improve his lot–for Shelly–and headed for an auction in Vermont. On the way, he stopped at a garage sale. Typical junk. But he noticed a workshop in the corner where an old man was reproducing antique furniture. When Carl showed an interest, the former cabinetmaker took him into the house crowded with precise reproductions of Colonial and Federal furniture. Pure eighteenth century workmanship. A pair of Philadelphia-style comb-back Windsor chairs caught Carl's eye and his imagination. With work on the patina, they could pass for the real McCoy, like those he'd seen at the art fraud exhibit at Boston's Museum of Fine Arts a few years ago. The exhibit had paired genuine antiques with frauds so convincing they'd fooled museum curators.

"I'm looking for something special for my wife's fiftieth birthday," he said. His ex-wife was forty-six. After a brief negotiation, the men settled at eight hundred for the pair of Windsors and a thousand for a tremendous pine corner cupboard.

On the way home, Carl stopped at a hardware store for a gallon of Quick Stripper, sandpaper, a rasp, towing chains, and a large potted geranium. Since the art fraud exhibit, Carl had read about other cases, as well as how to reapply patina on damaged antiques. Time to test himself, creating a finish so authentic no one would know—not Rachel, not Steven, not even a curator of American Decorative Arts.

First he glopped on the stripper and then scraped the finish off, careful to gouge the surface in a few places. He followed with the rasp and sandpaper. He imagined where shoes would've kicked during a thousand nights by the fire as he flattened out the turnings on the chair legs, and he burnished the spindles that fraction a wool jacket or a shirt would wear off over two hundred years. Then, strategically, he pounded the chairs with the towing chains. Finally, Carl lifted the geranium from its pot and shook dirt over each chair and rubbed it into the wood.

Over the next several days, he cleaned and oiled both chairs and rubbed in more dirt and ash and cleaned them again. He painted them black, added a coat of red, and finished with a loden green. Between each layer of paint, he worked with the chains, the rasp, and the sandpaper, revealing hints of the layered colors.

He also stripped the corner cupboard and slapped on a few coats of asparagus–green milk paint. As he labored, Carl sensed within himself something worn down, taken away, and something new added layer upon layer.

To age the paint and the wood of the chairs, he hauled them to the tip of Randolph Lake and buried them in the black boggy mud, marking the spot with Old Milwaukee beer cans he found in the woods.

In his workshop, Carl used square nails to refit the cupboard with antique lumber pillaged from an abandoned house, and he aged each cut and nail head with ash and dirt. Then he whacked the new wood of the cupboard with his chain, carved a child's initials into the side with a pen knife, and stippled a paste of dirt and ashes into the marks. With sandpaper in both hands, he massaged the wood, taking off six months wear with every touch, sanding down an edge where he imagined a woman's hip had swept the corner innumerable times on her way to the pantry. Carl also rubbed dirty motor oil around the knobs for two centuries worth of finger grease. He painstakingly reworked every detail and even broke off part of the molding at the top.

On the second evening, he went to the swamp and unearthed the chairs–they sucked out of the malodorous mud–he felt confident that they were ready for a final finish. In the morning, his fingers stroked the Windsors, around the slightly bowed comb which rolled down at the ends into a simple scroll, traced the gracefully tapered spindles from their pencil–thin tops down to the U–shaped brace arcing out into arms which ended in the scroll motif, inviting a flat–palmed grip. Through Carl's hands passed a perfect patina, a patina that inspired a mysterious provenance.

These chairs had been neglected for fifty years. No, seventy-five. By a once wealthy family, who, in their poverty, sold their valuables and set aside these chairs because . . . because they'd been left to a brother who died in World War I, and they remained in the barn. No–the attic. The attic of a Salem,

Massachusetts Federal home, one designed by Samuel McIntire. Too famous. Carl didn't want to invite research. *The chairs came from an old Rhode Island house. The name of the family had to remain unknown, the picker had insisted. Because the pride of blue-blood Yankees often outlasts their wealth. But if you knew Rhode Island history, the picker had assured Carl, you'd know the name. These Windsors with their broad seats, carved like a saddle, were no doubt familiar to famous family friends Ben Franklin and John Adams or so legend had it.*

Once more Carl cleaned and oiled the chairs. Nothing betrayed their age. They were better than those he'd seen at the art fraud exhibit. If anyone found fault with his chairs, who could blame Carl Packer, a man ignorant of fine antiques?

Loading the chairs into the van, he left to complete his pretext. He had to make a day-long picking trip, nosing around antique shops and yard sales in southeastern Massachusetts, making himself noticed.

The trip yielded the typical rubbish. With one exception. He found a professionally-repaired, twelve-inch Rookwood vase, a production piece. Its cranberry-colored top changed to green around a bulbous base of raised, stylized leaves, and XXI (for 1921) was stamped into the bottom under the logo. Worth eight hundred if perfect, it was a bargain at seventy. Even with the repair, Carl figured he could double his money. But the real prize he would tell the Portsmouth dealer, Steven Hale, were two spectacular Windsors he bought that afternoon from a Rhode Island picker he'd met in Seekonk, Massachusetts.

At Steven's home, a large brick Federal on Front Street, Carl rapped the brass knocker, then scratched his nose and smoothed his small bald head with suddenly cold hands. Steven Hale welcomed him as one welcomes money. In the garage, Steven studied the chairs by inches, and Carl watched the younger dealer struggle to hide his excitement. Carl pocketed his quivering hands and felt his heart pounding in his neck, certain Steven would notice these nicks in his varnish of composure.

If Steven discovered the truth, Carl made ready to laugh and say, I wagered that you'd know these were repros. You've got the best eye in the business, friend.

Then Steven stood up, dusting the knees of his khakis and re-tucking his blue Oxford shirt. "What do you want for them, Carl?"

"Make me an offer."

"You don't have a price?"

"I just got them and was excited to show you. Hadn't considered price."

"I'm interested, and I'd like to buy them. Tonight. How does five thousand sound?"

Carl looked at him for a split second, poker-faced. He had him. In that instant, his fear and distaste for deception vanished. "Before I respond to that figure, I just want to make sure we're on the same page. I assume you're talking per-chair and twice the money, right?"

Now it was Steven's turn to pause, his hand stroking the comb of one chair. "Well . . ." –a little sigh, half-raised eyebrows, and the angular nod of acceptance– "Okay, Carl. Ten thousand for both."

"I seem to remember," Carl Packer's eyes roamed the ceiling– this was fun now–and he held his chin, "a recent Sotheby's cata-log where *one* chair, almost identical to these two, sold for sixteen thousand–"

"Yeah, but that–"

"That chair had a great provenance. If this pair had an equal provenance, they'd bring, what? Forty? Fifty?"

"In New York, maybe. With two robber-baron collectors in a grudge match. But we're in New Hampshire, Carl. And we don't know this picker. Maybe he stole the chairs."

"If they were stolen, the museum would've gotten the word out."

"Museum? I admit they're good, but museum quality?"

Carl shrugged. "You know, I'm not ready to sell them tonight anyway. I think it's only fair that Rachel Goodson have a look."

When Carl started to lift a chair, Steven's hands grounded it, gently but firmly. "Hold on, Carl. We're friends. That's why you're here. Ten thousand is not enough, okay. I may be crazy, what with no real provenance, but I'm willing to give you fifteen for the pair right now. Tomorrow, I swear, not a penny more."

"But tonight, maybe seventeen?"

Steven shook his head. "Is that your price? Will that end this?"

Carl smiled. And Steven went to get his checkbook.

The next morning, over a bowl of corn flakes, Carl waited for the phone to ring. At nine o'clock Rachel Goodson called to say she was "disappointed" in Carl for not showing her the chairs first or giving her a chance to improve on Steven's offer.

"To make it up to you, Rachel," Carl said, "I'll show you a nifty corner cupboard Steven hasn't seen. It's from the same picker and the same Rhode Island family."

She offered to come over immediately.

"No, no." He couldn't risk her smelling the paint and stripper in his workshop. "I've got to load it up anyway. Thought I'd show Richard Sears in Boston."

"Oh, you don't want to drive all the way down there."

"Oh, I just might." As Carl yammered about what a fine dealer Richard Sears was, he pictured Rachel, her half-eye reading glasses perched at the end of her aristocratically thin nose, and dressed in her ruffled blouse and a long skirt like someone from the past, but she was shrewd as tomorrow. With every word of Richard Sears, Carl felt her urgency climb. "Just the same, I'll bring it by before I head for Beantown. Okey-doke?"

When Rachel saw it, she blurted out that it was the best corner cupboard she'd seen in ages. She marveled over the patina, rubbing it with reverent hands. In his typical honest fashion, Carl pointed out that he thought the back, while old, might not be original, and he showed her the broken molding.

She asked about the provenance and the picker. By this time, Carl recited the story so well it had the ring of truth. Finally she said, "Well, I like it. Can I save you a trip to Boston?"

"Depends."

"What do you need for it?" she asked, climbing on a footstool and lifting her glasses to study the molding.

"Twelve."

"Twelve hundred's a fair price."

"Twelve thousand."

She stumbled off the footstool. "Twelve thousand dollars? I couldn't get that from my craziest collector."

"You just said it's the best you'd seen in ages."

"True enough, but it's not worth twelve thousand, Carl. It's not. It's just not."

"Okay," he said, tracing an edge where the patina looked particularly rich, "I wanted to show Richard Sears anyway, and Steven Hale would appreciate a look."

"You're just wasting gas if you think Sears'll give you twelve. Or Steven either. If I could get fourteen, or even thirteen, I'd give you twelve in a heartbeat. But I can't."

"Well, you think about what you can afford, Rachel. It's only an hour to Bost–"

"It's not a matter of what I can afford." Her face went red above her ruffles, and he took pleasure in seeing her irked about money. "But I won't pay more than a thing is worth. I won't. I've got to turn a profit on every piece."

"I understand," Carl nodded. "You know what Steven said after paying a tad more for those chairs than he wanted? He said occasionally a top dealer has to pay top dollar to get quality merchandise and keep it from the competition."

"That's the difference between me and Steven," Rachel blustered, jabbing the air with her glasses. "I like him, but that young man throws money around to buy his reputation. Me, I've earned mine over thirty years in this business, and my customers know . . ." She was off to the races and Carl let her run.

They settled on nine thousand.

Carl tallied his profit. He paid eighteen hundred for the chairs and cupboard, two hundred for supplies, so in three weeks, he'd cleared twenty-four, just twelve grand short of what he made all last year.

That night, he worried about being discovered. While Steven could be silenced with cash and warnings of how he'd look for being fooled, Rachel would lock on like a snapping turtle until Carl went to jail. Even if his alibi survived, claiming he'd unwittingly bought frauds, his reputation as a knowledgeable and honest dealer would evaporate.

For all the times Steven and Rachel had fleeced him—oh sure, he'd made money from them but a pittance compared to their bonanzas—he deserved a little success at their expense. Who were the chumps now? Besides, they'd make money on the deal with their lists of rich collectors. So where was the harm? If anyone got plucked, it was the rich, and they had feathers to spare.

An hour later, he was still awake. The twenty-four thousand wasn't worth tarnishing himself. Honesty had been his stock in trade—knowledge and honesty. People took him at his word because his word *meant* something. There was comfort in integrity, if not much profit. Now that he'd covered Shelly's first years at UNH, Carl resolved never to cheat again.

Yet, as he settled himself against his pillow, he imagined another trip to the Vermont cabinetmaker. Towing a U–Haul. A big one.

*

Carl could hardly stand his shop now, surrounded by junk, making a buck here a buck there. When a woman came in, a tourist visiting the historic houses in Strawberry Banke, he had to roust himself to ask if she was looking for anything in particular. He started when she mentioned Rookwood pottery.

"Funny you should ask. I just found a piece. Haven't even priced it yet." From the cluttered storage room, he fetched the repaired vase. "If not for that—" He checked his inclination to point-out the repair. A sudden glossy darkness swelled inside him like the drawers of a bow-front chest. "If not for laziness, I'd have priced it and sold it by now."

"It's lovely," the woman said, her finger tracing where the cranberry mixed with the green of the base. "My grandmother worked for Maria Longworth Nichols at Rookwood, so I buy a piece once in a while."

"You're a serious collector?" Carl asked, recalling how some poured lighter fluid over pottery to reveal repairs.

"No, I just like it," she said. "How much is it?"

"For a vase in this pristine condition, the book says. . ." He opened a pottery pricing guide. The repair was a good one. A casual collector would never notice it. ". . . eight hundred dollars." With the repair it was worth perhaps a hundred and fifty. *Caveat emptor*, he thought. "But how does six sound?"

As the woman turned it in her hands, Carl gave voice to what he knew she was thinking, "Maybe your grandmother made that very vase." She nodded.

Right then the door banged open, shattering the moment. It was Rachel Goodson. Carl wanted to flee out the side door, but her cheerful voice calmed him, "Yoo-hoo, Carl."

"Rachel, what a surprise." Carl swept around the counter to intercept her before she saw the vase and revealed the repair.

"Just wanted to let you know I sold that cupboard today. Shipping it out to a Los Angles movie producer— What a lovely Rookwood vase." Rachel's undeniable hands reached out, "May I?"

The customer surrendered it, with Carl explaining, "Rachel is among New England's most respected antique dealers, selling to collectors, museums, celebrities, everywhere."

Rachel ran her thumb over the repair. She was going to nail him. But when she looked up, did he detect the slightest smile? "Fine workmanship, don't you think, Carl?"

They both knew she meant the repair. "Exceptional." His voice hitched and his scalp tingled like crazy.

Shyly the tourist asked, "Would you take five hundred?"

If he was out on this limb, he might as well dance on it. "Since I got a deal on it, and since your grandmother worked at Rookwood," he said magnanimously, "I think I could let it go for five."

Rachel browsed while the tourist wrote a check. Carl marveled at how easily, how naturally, he had pulled it off. Under his veneer of honesty, a rich dark grain had waited to shine all along. As if it were worth eight hundred dollars, Carl stuffed the vase with tissue paper and wrapped layers of padding around it.

After the woman left, Rachel Goodson said, "You must've done pretty well on that piece."

"Pretty good day," he hedged.

"Let me make it better." She paused. "If you get anything else from your Rhode Island picker," yes, she was smiling, "and I'm sure you will," she held forth a piece of paper, a folded check, "I want to see it first."

Carl opened the check: ten-thousand dollars.

"Half of that is an advance on my next purchase, half is a commission for the last cupboard and the next one. The next one must be identical, as if from the same room. Or quite different. Either way, it has to be as good in every detail as the last one, as good as Steven's chairs."

There might be sleepless nights ahead, but he could live with them. Successful men carried sins. At the age of fifty, this understanding came to him late, but now, as he slipped Rachel's check into his left shirt pocket and reached out to shake her hand, he saw how a life of choices had composed his human patina and Carl Packer was prepared to remake his.

A Pumpkin Summer

There I sat, perched on the edge of the toilet watching from the dark, second-floor window, watching at 2:26, 2:27, 2:28 in the morning, watching for Matt to sneak cross the property line and invade my pumpkin patch. I didn't know what he was up to but I knew he was up to something. Matt Baker was a neighbor and a deacon, but he was a Boston lawyer first. Willing to do anything to win at anything. Even a pumpkin-growing contest.

Matt's feigned nonchalance—the way he let his little girls water his pumpkins and hardly glanced at them when his Grand Cherokee steamed into the driveway at the day's end—all of that was a subterfuge. If there was one thing I had mastered as minister of the Congregationalist Church of Concord Massachusetts over the last ten years (and growing up as a preacher's kid, a PK), it was how to recognize a hypocrite. And I was going to sit at the bathroom window until Matt showed his true colors. I imagined Matt slipping from the sheets of the king–size bed–leaving Carol, her blonde hair a feathery muss on the pillow, her nightie hiked up around her thin waist to reveal her nicely rounded peach, and Matt not even noticing–to creep out the back door to sabotage my pumpkins. And the sabotage was subtle. My pumpkins were not withering on the vine, were not smashed or choked or blighted or slashed. I believed he slowly poisoned my pumpkins, perhaps using liquid detergent or bleach to chemically burn the root ends, as sensitive and tender as a baby's eyes. Maybe he pissed on them in the middle of the night. But when I got down on my hands and knees to sniff around the roots, it never smelled of urine, or bleach, or liquid Tide.

In a lucid moment, I wondered how I had come to sit here in the middle of the night–like a Roman sentry watching over pumpkins? What would I say if Nancy walked in and saw me peering out the window? A man of God stood above this. I could not imagine Dad, in this situation. Though he'd sat on this toilet.

Even ten years after Dad had called me down from my small Worthington, New Hampshire church (a church I loved) to pass the mantle of Concord Congregational and then retire to Arizona, it still felt like Dad's house, the house where I grew up. At any moment I expected to round a corner and collide with my father–forehead bumping his hard Windsor knot. An apology prepared. And it still felt like Dad's job, his church, his congregation, his deacons.

In Worthington life had been simpler; the congregation was simpler to be sure. Nancy and I were closer there. We laughed more, had more fun. And I felt less bottled up. Though I knew it a stereotype, I saw in Concord the crowning principles of wealth, materialism, and white liberals huddled away from Boston's urban strife–all swirling in contradiction to Christian faith.

During my second year at Concord, I had selected a spring Sunday to challenge the congregation. I spoke of how Jesus, who could have walked with anyone, chose to walk among the poor. I spoke of the obligation of the rich to reach out, tried to spur some noblesse oblige, tried to awaken the congregation to the systemic suppression so ingrained that we Americans see it as a birthright, somehow ordained by God, as if Jesus had outlined capitalism as a Christian model for the world. But Jesus had shared the fish and bread!

In a flash of inspiration, I had pointed to the organ, installed a few years before I took over for Dad, and asked what if the church had raised that $400,000 to build a home for welfare mothers? The congregation stirred, and I knew I'd finally struck the emotional chord. But at the end of the sermon, I went to the front door to greet parishioners as always, and they filed past me as if I did not exist.

Nancy pulled me aside after most of the congregation left.

"What were you thinking?" came her harsh whisper.

"What? It's my job to question things, to get people to think."

She pulled me into a side office and shut the door. "I can't believe you singled out the donation from Richard Ames before the entire congregation like that," she said. "It could cost you your job."

I swear I didn't know Richard Ames had donated the organ–I said as much to Nancy, but I don't think she believed me. Ames was a prominent church family for many generations, and Richard was a close advisor to my father. Or maybe I knew but forgot in the moment because I'd remembered the $400,000 amount. Either way Nancy was right, it could cost me my job.

Despite Nancy coaching me to do some damage control right away–and even offered to help me script my mea culpa–urging me to reach out to the deacons as well as preparing an apology to the Ames family and one to Richard individually, I did nothing. All week I prayed against experience that the incident might just go away. In reality, I felt too ashamed and worried to face my blunder.

The following Sunday, a third of the congregation stayed home in a kind of silent protest.

At the next deacon's meeting, three of the old guard had resigned (which had made room for Matt and two other young, wealthy, conservatives). The other nine lined up to blast me. They didn't care that I didn't know the $400,000 organ was donated by Richard Ames. They said it was my job to know such things. And they were right on that point. These businessmen saw parishioners as customers without whom there was no money to run the factory.

Still idealistic in those days, I tried to articulate that I saw them as souls to be saved.

"Hard to save them if they aren't there, wouldn't you say, Reverend?"

The deacons made it clear that to keep my job, I had to support the community. The way my father had. The good people of Concord loved their children, worked hard, and gave to charity. More deserving of commendation than a simple-minded attack. They did not attend church to be reformed. If I wanted to change the world, I could start by changing churches. Simple as that. The deacons expressed dismay that any of this was unclear to someone who'd grown up here, especially the son of Reverend Whitmyer.

I wanted to stand and proclaim, *I am Reverend Whitmyer.* But my tongue seized up as I imagined their retort: 'Oh, how we wish you were.'

Walking home from that deacons meeting, I stewed. I knew I was lucky to have the prestigious job. Wouldn't have it but for my father. Wouldn't have survived that meeting either. The weight of failure, of disappointing Dad, of uprooting my family, daunted. Once ousted, it was hard to land another church. In the time it took to plod the five blocks home, I decided to bend. Nancy and the kids loved Concord: historic, beautiful, prosperous, good schools, safe. Not to mention stifling, stagnant, and suffocating.

Since that fateful meeting with the deacons eight years ago, I logged seven days a week. Much of my time went to budgeting time: managing a wall calendar, a stupid Google calendar on my stupid smartphone, and one on my computer; scheduling visits and meetings, making to-do lists, writing reminders, and checking or adjusting all of these in addition to creating sermons. The routine had become maddening.

Until the pumpkins. As soon as the infant plants emerged from black potting soil, I knew the Lord had blessed me with tremendous gourds. A mini-miracle right there in the musty basement of my Concord, Massachusetts parsonage. Suddenly something new and full of promise filled my life. Under my care bloomed measurable change, growth, improvement. Three times daily I watered my pumpkins: moderately soaking at mid-morning and mid-afternoon, heavily soaking in the evening. Exactly at noon, I fed them a special fertilizer, a secret potion of my own design, and poured it over the plants. This concoction combined the published secrets of renowned horticulturists as well as the sparse but seminal works on the succor of giant pumpkins. My growth potion consisted of milk, cow dung, peeled banana, eggs (with shells), sugar, a teaspoon of fish food, and small clippings of human hair. Into the food processor these items went to form a creamy, verdant-colored soup which had a fecund smell both sweet and sour, an odor that more than once nearly drew my lips to the edge for a taste.

The *routine* of work, it seemed, had become more important than Faith. When had I last reflected on what it meant to be a Man-of-Faith for more than three minutes?

From the pulpit I still longed to shout: Who among you would unplug your cable TV, hand over the keys to your four-wheel-drive grocery-getter, or send your children to a mere community college if it meant saving one African child from starvation?

But then, what did that have to do with Faith? Humanity, yes. But Faith? I seemed to have lost the ability to connect the dots.

The calling had become toil. I trudged through knee-deep snow steadfastly but without any sense of destination in my assignment to guide these rich people, these master rationalizers and exploiters, through the eye of a needle. In weaker moments, I waxed for a bigger piece of the pie myself. And there were more, weaker moments all the time. Those reveries certainly lasted more than three minutes.

A year ago, I reached for a piece of the pie and requested a $30,000 raise from the deacons, a fraction of what the twelve well-heeled men who owned my fate drew in annual bonuses. I presented statistics showing that Concord ranked among the most expensive cities in New England, making it one of the more expensive in the nation. Matt, the big-shot Boston lawyer who chaired the Finance Committee, led the rebuff. He recalled that my salary exceeded the average for my career. (Not his.) He pointed out that I paid nothing to live in a home easily worth a million dollars, equal to about a $5,000 monthly mortgage payment, which translated into $60,000, tax free, lifting my salary "in real terms" well beyond a minister of my experience. I might have argued about the house, what with the work the drafty old barn needed as well as how I missed the tax advantage and investment of home ownership. But Matt, the marksman, had already blasted my hope out of the sky. Nothing but a puff of feathers drifting earthward. Leaving the other deacons to stomp whatever life was left in the idea. One old deacon hunched over his stupid smartphone calculator, thick fingers pounding the buttons, confirming Matt's numbers in more exact terms.

In the end, I got a four percent cost-of-living increase. And I thanked them for it.

*

"Get back. Get back," I ordered my kids. They hovered at my elbows as I bent under the growth lamp to drip water around each pale green stem.

"Can I do one?" Gordon asked.

"Me too," Megan chimed.

"No. You'd kill them with too much water," I warned.

From across the cellar came an assertive crack of wet pants. Nancy, again doing laundry, had pulled jeans from the washer and gave them a hard shake before dashing them into the dryer.

"Soon you can water them. But let's give them time to grow. Okay, kids?"

Another snap of pants before Nancy sent the kids to wash up for dinner.

I didn't like what was coming. Nancy dropped the laundry basket at my feet and spoke in a whisper. "What's with you, Peter? We bought those seeds for the kids, and now you bully them aside like ... like a toy train collector who won't let his kids touch a caboose. Loosen up."

"I'm trying to assure a good experience by getting the seedlings to a place where the kids can help." It sounded lame even as I said it. "Besides, a lot of money is at stake. First prize at the Topsfield Fair won over $16,000 last year." That this would help replace the raise I'd requested was not lost on me.

"Oh, Peter. . ." Nancy rolled her eyes. "First of all, you're a minister, not a master pumpkin grower. Second, we'll survive without the $16,000. Third, there's a relationship with your kids at stake."

"You exaggerate."

"Think about it, Peter. How many chances do you get to connect with them? I mean *really* connect?"

Point made.

"This is a chance to connect." She picked up the laundry basket. "Don't blow it." She bumped me with the basket as she passed. I believed it deliberate but let it go without a word.

Nancy made sense–her and her first, second, and third points held over from high school debating days–but those seedlings whispered to me.

And they whispered to me still as I sat at the bathroom window a half an hour later–2:56, 2:57, 2:58–still no sign of that lawyer. Maybe Matt didn't invade every night. Subtle though it might be, the sabotage was real. Craving revenge, I decided to act.

I slipped downstairs, careful not to wake Nancy, and pulled on my navy blue Gordon Conwell Theological Seminary sweatshirt in the kitchen. Then I plucked a knife from the woodblock on the counter. In a military crouch, I ran across the back yard, feeling the lawn go smooth and thick underfoot when I crossed into Matt's Chemlawn–perfect yard (the deacons allocated money for Chemlawn only on my front yard). Near the pumpkin patch, I dropped to my belly and crawled army–style through the dirt to Matt's largest pumpkin so hefty I couldn't wrap my arms around it. Frequently giant pumpkins split and collapsed under their own weight. So no one would suspect this. Breathing as hard as a sprinter, I lay three hairline slashes in the folds of the smooth orange skin. The cuts, about an inch deep, should split the pumpkins in a few days. Sweat ran down my temples in the warm night air. I resisted the impulse to chew through the vine like an animal. I belly-crawled to the next two largest pumpkins and put the blade to them. Tempted to slash all five of the big ones, I feared arousing suspicion and let the others go.

Then I heard something. A door. I lay flat in the dirt, hiding behind one of the pumpkins I'd slashed. Had someone seen me? Was it Matt, sneaking out to attack my pumpkins? Then I saw Carol standing by the pool in a white terrycloth robe. She studied the water. Then, as graceful as a dancer, she bent one knee and swept her other foot into the water, testing the temperature. My chest burned from holding my breath, and I let it out, breathing through my mouth in short chops. She paused at the shallow end, looking

around. Her gaze seemed to fall on me and linger. The look of
desire. Then she dropped her robe and lifted her nightgown over
her head. For a moment she stood naked in the moonlight and
then lowered herself down the steps into the pool.

I fought the urge to lick the smooth, firm skin of pumpkin next
to my face. Perhaps she knew I was there and wanted me. What
if I walked over? "Oh, it's you. I thought some kids had sneaked
into your pool." What then? She might invite me to join her. And
I would. And she would swim to me, and wrap her arms around
my neck, her small breasts pressing to my chest, and wrap her
legs around my waist. Her lips meeting mine. Her tongue, a little
animal, inviting me inside. Her tongue. And her legs drawing our
hips tight. Her eyes widening and then thinning in a smile. That
passion unlocked.

I pressed my erection into the ground. Fear held me there.

Soon Carol emerged from the pool, water flowing down her
body, glistening in the scant light. How I wished for more illumi-
nation. She squatted to lift her robe and drew it around herself.
Then she retrieved her nightgown and carried it inside.

Had she put on this display for me? Her gaze had lingered in
my direction.

I crawled out of Matt's pumpkin patch and scurried home. In
the kitchen, I pulled off the dirty sweatshirt, and the first wave of
guilt hit me in the gut. What had I done? Rash as water, I'd flushed
reason. Was this the act of a reverend? A man of God? My mouth
dry, I poured a glass of water and sat at the table. The easy maxims
surfaced: Do unto others… Revenge is mine saith the Lord… But I
had planned a retaliation for days, and without evidence. I lowered
my head to my hands and prayed for forgiveness. Then I raised
up, polished off the water, and went to bed.

*

By late August my fertilizer had kicked in, and my top three pumpkins were huge and swelling measurably by the day. Matt's three largest pumpkins had split open. Their exposed pulp turned into a black gel and the gaping edges grew fuzzy with green-and-white mold. Wracked with guilt at the sight of these rotting carcasses, I fought a nagging sense of obligation to confess to Matt. But how could I? He'd laugh in my face at the absurdity of his minister-neighbor's overblown desire to grow a bigger pumpkin and how it turned me into a pumpkin slasher. Though I preached that a Christian need ask the Lord's forgiveness but once, my own kitchen-table prayer assuaged nothing. While tending pumpkins, "Father, forgive me," kept bubbling up. No echo of clemency, no exculpation, radiated back from the heavens like radar waves to cleanse my black gel of guilt. Until it came, I kept asking. Matt's other big pumpkins looked healthy and might be top-twenty contenders at the Topsfield Fair in October. The best way to mitigate my guilt was to focus on my own pumpkins, especially the one I'd named Schwartz (after a crotchety Old Testament professor I'd had). It was a monster, bigger than a bean-bag chair now. If hollowed out, my ten-year-old son could hide inside. I was pretty sure Schwartz was as large as last year's record-breaker, maybe bigger.

I spent more time with my pumpkins as they matured into a mellow orange, sitting among them on a low beach chair the way a dog breeder might sit among his hounds, the champion at his side. (From that position, I still caught frequent glimpses of Carol working among her flowers.) It dawned on me that the pumpkins could become a career. I schemed of generating a lucrative market for giant pumpkins. One in every bank branch and hotel lobby. Trigger corporate competition to display the largest pumpkin, paying hundreds or thousands for each one. I imagined naming my business: Peter Peter Pumpkin Breeder. I'd buy a farm and become the Orville Redenbacher of pumpkins. Preaching the gospel of roasted pumpkin seeds as the hot snack of the new millennium. Try our new barbecue flavor! With guerrilla marketing, personal evangelizing, and then a frontal media assault, pumpkin pie could overthrow apple as America's favorite. And someday a biography would tell how the one-time reverend turned pumpkin mogul when he discovered his genius in a small pumpkin patch in his Concord, Massachusetts back yard and how he snatched the national spotlight with Schwartz, the world's largest pumpkin. A nutty idea maybe, but big things start small. I reached out to pat Schwartz and rub the smooth, firm skin.

Nancy had said, "For God's sake, Peter, it's just a pumpkin." Then accused me of caring more about Schwartz than her or the children. Nonsense, I'd replied. But I did love Schwartz. In the harsh glare of honesty, what Nancy failed to see was that the great pumpkin had not produced itself, this tremendous fruit had not come to fruition by itself. Schwartz was an extension of me, of my latent talent. I had discovered my calling. And there was something spiritual about it. I now ranked among the world's foremost pumpkin growers. It was the only first-class, even world-class, thing I'd ever done. In school, I was a lousy athlete and an above-average student. As a minister, I moiled in Dad's shadow, competent but largely inert. With Schwartz it was different. Thousands at the Topsfield Fair would stand in awe of my creation. With Schwartz–let the cynics call it mere pumpkin growing–I had a shot at greatness. In this, I left Matt (who was but one of thousands of Boston lawyers), and even my distinguished father, far behind.

*

Wednesday afternoon before the fair, I walked home from a meeting of the Women's Auxiliary, finally free of the lingering old ladies and their rose essence as well as their fond remembrances of my father. As I walked up the driveway, I saw Matt standing over Schwartz. I suppressed my instinct to protect Schwartz, ordering Matt back, back, back like a yapping poodle or an old woman shooing a goat from the garden.

"Just admiring your pumpkins, especially this one here," he indicated Schwartz, "a real brute. You know," Matt said, "I've been thinking about how to lift these giants into a trailer for the fair." For weeks I'd worried about moving Schwartz without a Humpty Dumpty scene. Matt had an ingenious idea, which we decided to test on one of his pumpkins.

We went to U-Haul and rented an open-air trailer and drove to the hardware store to buy a soft canvas drop cloth for a sling. Matthew insisted on paying for it all because I'd provided the seeds. On the way back, I used Matt's cell phone to recruit a few strong young men from church to heft the practice pumpkin. Then came Matthew's stroke of genius. Raiding Carol's stocking drawer, we plundered a dozen pairs of pantyhose: sheer, black, navy, white, tan. We stretched the legs of the panty hose around the pumpkin, knotting them at the ankles to give the pumpkin support, using as many pairs from as many angles as possible. During the process, I imagined Carol's shapely legs filling out these nylons and noted the little cotton crotch.

The plan worked.

On Friday, we loaded the others. When lifting Schwartz, I took pleasure in the straining necks of the men who lifted the tremendous pumpkin into the trailer. There in the middle, surrounded by Matt's three pumpkins, Schwartz ruled.

*

Morning brought a fall day from the cover of an L.L. Bean catalog, foliage in screaming colors, a cool snap to the air but warm sunshine. The air smelled fresh, tinged with that dank scent of fallen leaves. The glory of the morning foreshadowed my crown as the world's greatest pumpkin grower. Carol pranced out with two boxes of doughnuts and put them on the hood of the Grand Cherokee. Nancy trucked out coffee–and was pleased that everyone liked her pumpkin-spice version. She also made pumpkin-spice hot chocolate. Meanwhile, Matt threw a Nerf football for the kids, the old quarterback remembering game days like this one. His girls were better athletes than my kids.

I paced back and forth from the doughnuts on the hood of the SUV to the trailer where I could admire Schwartz. I ate three doughnuts and bit into a fourth before I knew it. Brushing some dirt off of my massive pumpkin, I remembered a ploy I'd considered: taking a large syringe and needle to pump water or gel into Schwartz to add weight. But I didn't for fear of splitting and because I couldn't imagine a pumpkin more colossal than Schwartz—twice the size of a beanbag chair now.

I barked at the kids for climbing on the trailer to retrieve the football when it nearly hit Schwartz, and Carol chirped, "Oh, Peter, they won't hurt your baby."

That shut me up. But it didn't keep me from taking a fourth doughnut—or was it a fifth?—and leaning up against the trailer to stand guard.

At the fairgrounds, we pulled into the barn where the great pumpkins were weighed. In his newish bib overalls, plaid flannel shirt, and clean baseball cap, the scale supervisor had to be an insurance agent or a local bank vice president in costume. "Boy, that one in the middle is a monster. Looks like we got us a contender." Then he clucked for the "fellas" to come over to hoist the pumpkins out of the trailer.

A front end loader lifted Schwartz onto the scales and Mr. Bib Overalls slid the weights to 2,000 pounds and the needle didn't budge. Ha. At 2,210, the needle floated, and my heart dipped. I wanted to thumb the scale, wished I hadn't rubbed off that bit of dirt this morning. My heart thumped in my chest, and I held my breath. The scale's pound-slide kept going, 2,217, 2,219, 2,223 and it didn't stop until it hovered at 2,227 pounds—a new world record. Everyone sent up a cheer, and I couldn't help but beam and laugh.

Tears flowed before I could draw down my composure. I'd done it. In a single growing season, Peter Whitmyer, by the grace of God and gumption, became the greatest pumpkin grower in history.

We stayed to watch other pumpkins weighed, but none were close. I lingered in the spotlight with Schwartz, calculating my winnings: $5,000 prize plus $5 per pound to a grand total of $16,135.

Then a gleaming red pickup pulled in, and a crowd gathered. I pushed in and my knees went weak at the sight. Nestled in a bed of straw with carbuncle-like warts sat a blotchy, vile-looking mountain of a gourd that looked like it might bite.

The idiot in bib overalls did his best Green Acres: "Woo-wee, I do believe that big fella there's gonna break the scale." What it broke was my world record. It weighed 2,346 pounds, grown by the magician out of Salisbury, Mass. who'd set the world record a year before. I fought back tears of disappointment.

A new contest followed, one I didn't know about. Students from the Montserrat College of Art in Beverly carved the top fifteen pumpkins into jack-o-lanterns. I started to withdraw Schwartz, but Nancy put her foot down. "It's part of the event, and you're not going to spoil it."

I wanted to leave, but the kids had to see the jack-o-lanterns. So our group milled around the fair. First we went to the livestock barn to visit the pigs like hippos, steers the size of trucks, sheep you could saddle. Soon I mindlessly followed the pack, imagining some Gen-Z kid with an eyebrow ring and a pierced tongue taking a chainsaw and hatchet to Schwartz. The midway should have been fun, watching the kids on the hokey, rattletrap rides, except the operators looked creepy, like they might snatch a kid. More weirdoes at the games, where Matt demonstrated his athletic prowess by shooting a basketball into an impossibly small hoop to win a big pink teddy bear. Eventually we headed back to the pumpkins, passing through the garden barn: zucchinis as big as your thigh, strawberries the size of tennis balls, cabbages bigger

than your head. The whole fair I realized–Schwartz included–was
a freak show.

Concord too. With its enforcement of black–shuttered white
houses in town; the tucked–away strip malls; hidden dumpsters;
Ivy League postures. The whole town–and–country pretense. Un-
tenable for my soul, a decade wasted.

The jack–o–lantern contest was set up on a makeshift stage, curtain drawn. As we sat and waited, maudlin memories overtook me.
The first blossoms. How the base of each flower had swelled, slowly
forming infant pumpkins, green ping–pong balls. And how they'd
grown through the summer under my care (leaving an immense
water bill for the deacons to mutter about), getting huge. Becoming
Schwartz.

Okay, I didn't win, but I, Peter Whitmyer, had grown the world's
second–largest pumpkin in history–and I set the world record, if
only briefly. Despite the disappointment of not winning first prize,
it was a huge accomplishment. I had to give myself that. In my
first try, only one pumpkin in history grew larger than Schwartz,
and that from a man who'd been at it for many years.

Finally a professor from the art college, a man dressed in black
and too old for his shoulder–length pony tail, came out to emcee
the show. He talked about the giant jack–o–lanterns we were about
to see.

In the midst of the noise and anticipation, there I sat in a kind
of stillness and quiet, waiting for another wave of emotion, of joy
or sadness, to overtake me–like another wave curling to crash on
the beach.

When the curtain opened, people actually cheered.

Front and center, complete with horns and a tuft of crazy hair,
sat Schwartz with a vile smirk, carved into the devil. "Peter, it looks
like you," Carol shouted, laughing. I heard Jack and Nancy agree.

I looked at Schwartz. The resemblance was evident. What did it
mean, a devil? Or did it mean nothing more than Halloween fun?

Sometimes a cigar is just a cigar. There were other demons among the giant jack-o-lanterns. And a couple of clowns.

Before I could over-think it, I heard cutting through the crowd applause and cheer, a piercing full-bore laugh, an infectious guffaw that registered both familiar and bygone. It was Nancy. How long had it been since I'd heard her really cut loose and belt out that laugh? At one time, her laugh had liberated me. Back in college, so bottled up was I that this bellow—and the young woman behind it—had uncorked me. I remember after our second date, she coaxed me to break into the bell tower and climb to the top with her where we unabashedly haw-hawed over campus only to find two security guards waiting for us at the bottom. I looked at Devil Schwartz and a smirk bubbled up in me, a chortle, and finally a roar.

A Membrook Man

Five years ago, I was on the fast track as they used to say—an MBA grad at twenty-six; at thirty a vice president of Beacon Bank; at thirty-four head of the mortgage department and well into a six-figure income—busting my hump to break into the old-boy's network and everything going great, swimmingly, in my thirty-eighth year.

Until my older brother showed up.

His hammering at the back door interrupted our dinner of red snapper and artichokes. Julie and I glanced at each other across the table. She rolled her eyes, so I got up, thinking how awful cold artichokes taste. When I reached the kitchen, Jimmy had let himself in and stood there like a stray dog in a New England Patriots T-shirt and Red Sox cap. I felt a dull, honey–slow pain ebb down my left thigh at the sight of him. His heavy features billboarded his familiar, winning grin, a grin that had helped him dodge a lot of trouble over the years. Although we're both six feet tall, the low kitchen ceiling of our 250–year–old house, which always felt cozy to me, seemed to crowd my brother.

"Hey, bro," he said, jabbing an open palm toward me.

"Jimmy! Good to see you. What's up?" His grin and excessively firm handshake signaled danger. Unless he wanted something, I never heard from him, never saw him. His rank BO hit my nose.

He tipped the bill of his cap way back off his forehead and continued to grin as sweat ran down his temples. When Julie entered the kitchen, Jimmy gathered her up in his arms. "How's my favorite sister–in–law?"

"Your only sister–in–law," she said.

"Don't get bogged down in the details, Mrs. Membrook." And he pressed his lips to her forehead, humming as if tasting a dessert, and withdrew with a hearty smack. He kept an arm slung over her shoulder, and I noted her wincing from the smell.

Although she laughed, I read her glance as a request for intervention. Julie hardly knew my brother, having seen him perhaps a half a dozen times in our eight years of marriage: at our wedding, a Christmas, a Thanksgiving or two.

"So, Jimmy," I said, gently drawing his shoulder away from Julie, "what's up?"

She ducked his grasp and asked if she could get him something to drink.

"I'll always drink a banker's imported beer." Jimmy laughed and punched me in the shoulder. "And maybe take a dip in your hot tub." It made me wonder when he'd last showered.

In the living room, Julie rushed to preserve the off-white wing chair from my brother's dirty jeans. Jimmy dropped himself on the navy sofa and drew a long pull off his bottle of Bass Ale, ignoring the beer flute Julie had set out for him. "Ahh, nice brew, brother."

"I didn't hear you pull up," I said.

"Took the train and walked." He hoisted the bottle again.

"You should've called us to pick you up," Julie said.

"I didn't want to be any trouble," he answered. The statement hung between us like a noxious gas. Jimmy had more to say, and I waited to hear it. Instead, he pattered about how good it felt to get out of Boston. My 42-year-old brother's hands tunneled forward and spread wide as he described how the train shed the industrial wastelands and second-class suburbs for the fields and woods near Ipswich. "I could picture you, Rog, riding the train in your Brooks Brothers suit." After another long drink of beer, he explained how he'd had a dandy arrangement with a little old lady in East Boston; got so he didn't even mind the jets flying in and out of Logan. A sweet deal, he said, until the old woman suffered a stroke. A panic flickered in me. When her "vulture kids," as he called them, descended to claim her things and put the house up for sale, they wanted his back rent–but he'd lost his job because of "this sono-fabitch warehouse manager"–anyway, he told the vultures to stuff it where the sun don't shine. And they told him to hit the bricks. "So I'm on the street, you know," he said. "I stayed with friends for a little while, but it wore thin." He wove a tapestry of victim-hood: how his s.o.b. boss had made him a scapegoat and fired him, how the stinking cops towed his car because he forgot to pay a few lousy parking tickets, and how he didn't have the cash to pay back-tickets since he didn't have a frigging job. On and on he went like that, sounding like someone twenty-two, not forty-two.

My mind wandered, registering the sense but not the specifics of my brother's words. This conditioned response remained from growing up under the downpour of our father's rages about some injustice visited upon him. I remember turning away from Jimmy, looking out the window of my handsome living room where the sky, wavy through the antique glass, was turning the first peach shade of sunset. I thought of the grassy hilltop behind our house where I could watch the sun set over the fields and woods of Ipswich or could watch it dawn over the salt marshes. Although I seldom went up the hill, I often thought of it, picturing the majestic view, thinking I should lug my old telescope up there for a look at the planets and stars, but there was so little time after work in those days. At that moment, with the percussion of my brother's complaints pounding, and picturing the view, I had the urge to head for the hilltop.

My concentration was yanked back into the room when I heard Julie say: "You're family, Jimmy, of course you can stay with us."

Before I could kill the offer, Jimmy ran with it. Trotting out the clichés. "Julie and Roger, you guys are the best. You're what family is all about. I knew I could count on you two. Thick and thin, we Membrooks stick together." He hooted a laugh, flashing his big smile. He was buoyant, and I was sinking.

"This is only for a little while, couple months, three tops," he said. "Just till I get on my feet. I'm gonna find a good job, settle down, and buy a house." He read the doubt in my eye. "Yeah, me a homeowner. Just like you, Rog. Well, not just like you, because I can't afford a place like this, but a small house, a fixer-upper. And I'll pitch in around here. I'm pretty handy, you know."

"Yeah." I was already figuring out how to get rid of him and wondering what it would cost me to support another person.

"Now I can start fresh," his arms opened wide, wet circles under each, and swept the air, "right here, in beautiful Ipswich. Cause for celebration! But my beer's empty."

"Let me get you another," Julie said, and I heard her clear our cold red snapper and artichokes from the dining room table on her way to get my brother a beer.

"So, what's your plan?" I asked, rising to the edge of my chair.

"I don't do a lot of planning, Roger. You know that. You're the planner."

"So, if you don't have a plan," I said, "how're you going to improve your situation?"

"You sound like somebody's father." He chuckled and ducked his chin to his chest to belch. "I'll be ready when opportunity knocks. Maybe I'll win the lottery," he said. "Dollar or two a day for a chance to become a millionaire."

"So, you think you'll win the lottery?" I realized I was starting every statement with "so," but I couldn't help myself.

"Somebody's got to win. Why not me?"

"Millions of people lose so a few can win. That's the way it works, Jimmy. You stand a better chance of getting hit by lightning."

"Hey, people get struck by lightning every year," he said, pointing the barrel of his empty beer bottle at me like a gun. "And you don't get struck unless you're out in the rain, bro."

That damn grin.

Unable to stand it, I got up to leave. This was not how I wanted to talk to my older brother. Four years older, the old cliché said I was supposed to look up to him, but I never had. How could I? As kids growing up in Lawrence, Mass., he was always the better athlete, and he bullied me with years of punches, ear flicks, and Dutch rubs.

Late one night, after my father had caught my drunk brother trying to "borrow" a neighbor's car and roughed him up, Jimmy came in and tipped me out of bed by lifting one side of my mattress. He was eighteen, a senior in high school, and I was fourteen. I retaliated with a shove, and he unleashed a fury unlike any I'd seen. It culminated when he stopped kicking me on the floor and jumped on my left leg, snapping my femur.

I spent the next four months in a hip-high cast. After he broke my leg, Jimmy quit school, just two months before graduation, and left home. We lived in the top floor apartment of a meager three-family: 23 Sullivan Street. When he returned, he apologized by giving me a telescope, a good one. I thanked him, and he laughed.

"Don't be too thankful. I sold your bicycle to help pay for it." I blankly looked at him, waiting to hear that he was kidding, that he hadn't sold my most prized possession—a cherry-red, ten-speed Schwinn Varsity—the envy of my friends and the sole reason I'd delivered newspapers for three years. With a shrug he said, "You couldn't ride it this summer anyway. When you get well, you can have my old bike." His bike was a scratched and battered five-speed Huffy with no rear brakes and two flat tires. I hated his bike, but I loved the telescope.

I looked out the window at the moon and later hobbled to the roof of the apartment building, Jimmy shouldering the telescope for me, and I studied the stars and planets. The telescope lifted me above the world of my father's ranting and my mother's simmering subservience. Jimmy came and went during the next few years, vanishing without a word for a week or more. His disappearances worried my mother and enraged my father. In the absence of his real target, my father's rages ricocheted in all directions, and I took cover with my telescope. To flee the grimy world of Sullivan Street, I traced the predictable movement of the stars or focused on the lunar terminator, the line between light and dark on the moon's surface.

With my broken leg, I gave up sports and joined the astronomy club which revealed that education could change my life. I set my sights on earning an academic scholarship to college and did. At Holy Cross, I studied business and took a minor in astronomy. Meanwhile, my brother's life flowed into the rut created by a long line of Membrook men, bouncing from one menial job to another, never staying long enough to elevate his standing. An entry-level life.

Looking at his self-satisfied grin that night in my living room, I asked myself: why did he acquiesce to the world that inspired me to escape by bettering myself?

I had to get away from him, and I headed for the hill behind the house.

Outside the backdoor, I nearly tripped over two big, black garbage bags beside the rhododendron. They held the contents of my brother's life: clothes, trinkets, softball glove.

I quickened my pace for the hilltop.

Watching the June sunset, I realized I was biting my fingernails. I hadn't done that since high school, since I had last lived with Jimmy. He used to tease me about my nail biting. As dusk settled into twilight, the first stars showing, I still waited for a sense of peace. I wished I had my old telescope up there. Stored in the attic, I hadn't looked through it for years. Julie called me from the backdoor of our 1743 saltbox. I waited a bit longer, but the calm never came.

*

From bed that night, I listened to Jimmy sing in the shower.

"How could you say yes before we discussed it?" I asked Julie who worked in her face lotion. "I'd have said no. A flat, unequivocal, NO. He can't stay."

She turned to watch me stew. "I'm sorry. Even though you two have had your differences, I assumed you'd want to help your only brother." She went back to rubbing in the lotion. "Your only sibling."

"You and your: 'family's always welcome.'"

"I'm sorry."

"'Always,' always is the key word here. He may live with us that long, you know?"

"Roger," Julie said, getting in bed, "he's not staying more than three or four months."

"Four months? Now it's four months? By breakfast it'll be six months. This is like the legal system in reverse. You get sentenced to two months, but you get six for good behavior." After a few seconds, I muttered that he'd better get a job fast because I couldn't afford to carry him on my back for long.

"If money's so tight, why'd you buy that BMW? Why do we need that thing anyway? You take the train to work."

"You want to play with the big boys, you dress like the big boys."

"Why didn't you buy the smaller one?"

"The 325 is for wannabes. The 525 says you've arrived."

"But if we can't afford it—"

"We can't afford *not* to afford it. Trust me, these things have a way of paying for themselves." My wife—with her practical, middle-class background (daughter of a first-grade teacher and a pharmacist), a far better home than I'd grown up in, but well below what I had envisioned for us—was nonplused by these facts, first the house and more recently the car. But I had made a study of the men who inherited power and wealth, and they trusted those of their ilk. Had I driven a Volkswagen, worn cheesy suits, or lived in a ranch house, I'd have remained a paper shuffler under Emory Lambert, president of Beacon Bank.

"What I can't afford," I said punching my pillow, "is carrying the dead weight of a deadbeat."

Julie turned away to sleep. "I didn't realize how much you hate him."

Hate? Did I hate my brother? I listened to him leave the bathroom and rumble around in the guest room. Sounded like he was rearranging our furniture, scratching the wide pine floors. Then I heard him pulling his clothes from the black garbage bags. The jackal I once escaped had hunted me down and prowled outside my bedroom door.

Unable to avoid the thought as I lay there late at night, I realized I'd never quite gotten over Jimmy stealing my first girlfriend, Maggie. I was seventeen and Jimmy twenty-one. With charming magnetism, self-assurance, and legal access to all the booze Maggie wanted, he took her from me. Walking home from an astronomy club field trip to the University of Lowell, I saw my brother's Galaxy 500 parked in the shadow of the football stadium and thought he'd come to give me a ride, but when I approached, I discovered a shirtless Maggie necking with my brother, and an empty bottle of Boone's Farm Apple Wine on the dash. After that, I kept my girl-friends secret from my brother. He'd called me a faggot when I refused to talk about the girls I dated at college, but I laughed at him because I knew I was rocketing beyond his reach. Eventually, I had imagined, I would have to look back, down and back, through time with my telescope to even remember what Jimmy Membrook looked like.

But then, after I'd become a thirty-eight-year-old banker, fol-lowing a decade of mixing with the Yankee blue bloods, learning their ways, and soaring light years above my beginnings, Jimmy tracked me down and moved into my house. Now he slept one bedroom away from my wife and me, and I wondered if he might try something with Julie. How easily he had bundled her into his arms that evening and made her laugh. And how quickly she seemed to defend him.

The next morning, Julie suggested having Jimmy live with us wouldn't be so bad, a chance for brothers to reconnect. I smiled at her sentimental sales pitch and thought how my whole life had been about escaping the Membrook legacy. She kissed my fore-head and said, "I love you."

"Love you too," I responded, but my attention shifted to the sound of the toilet flush in the hall bathroom.

*

Within two weeks, Jimmy got a job as a yard ape at Ipswich Lumber, a summer position. Then, just as I had suspected, he asked to borrow money to get his car back. Unpaid parking tickets, tow-ing fee, and storage charges came to $800. Probably more than the clunker was worth. Reluctantly (fearing he'd borrow my BMW and return it with a creased fender like he did with my Datsun B210 when he came to visit me at Holy Cross, insisting it was hit while parked in the lot), I loaned him the cash. And the next day his rust-bucket of a Chevy was parked outside our house.

When not at the lumberyard, he helped Julie at her antique shop or worked around the house. One night neither of them were at the house when I got home late, and I went to see if they were at the shop.

There in the last shop window still aglow on Main Street, they sat together, speckled with mustard-yellow paint, sitting close on one of those small sofas laughing and clinking Bass Ale bottles together. It was a moment more intimate than any I'd shared with my wife since Jimmy moved in. For months Julie had been after me to help her paint that wall of her shop, and though I'd promised to help, I kept putting her off. The spectacular wedding set I'd bought her the first year my salary passed $140,000 was, like the rest of her fingers, covered with yellow paint. It was like her to forget to take the rings off. I stayed in the shadows outside watching them. For a long time I watched them—wishing I too had yellow paint on me—as they talked and drank and laughed and admired the result of their teamwork. I expected them to lock in a romantic embrace any second. Then Julie looked at her watch, another gift from me that would require cleaning, and realized how late it was and they started washing up. That's when I drove home.

Around the house Jimmy oiled hinges, cleaned and treated the wood gutters with boiled linseed oil, repainted shutters, and such. If he weren't so damn useful, I might have booted him. Of course, when he cut the grass, he hit a rock and broke my mower. And the next week, Jimmy fertilized the yard right after I'd fertilized it. So while the houses on our street featured lush lawns like something out of *Better Homes and Gardens*, ours turned brown, dead as the surface of the moon. Although he swore it was an accident, I believed he did it on purpose, trying to knot my gut at the sight of my chemically scorched lawn, trying to make me look bad to the neighbors, trying to drag me down to his level.

One night Julie and I relaxed in the hot tub, wearing bathing suits because the neighbors could see us–my springs just loosening up–when I heard Jimmy's Chevy careen into our driveway, splashing gravel into the dead grass. Dirty and sweaty from a game with the lumberyard softball team, and three-sheets-to-the-wind from the post–game celebration, he ripped off his clothes and paused in the nude to flex his muscles and pound his ample belly (penis wagging in the evening light). Then he screamed a war cry and leaped into the hot tub. Julie couldn't stop laughing. "A bathing suit, Mrs. Membrook? I'm surprised. And disappointed." My buck-naked brother proceeded to swim laps around the tub–crawling over Julie and me as he went–and tested how long he could hold his breath underwater. I recalled stories of people drinking in hot tubs and suffering heart attacks. But I knew his heart was healthy as a diesel.

Jimmy's help-yourself mentality resembled a high school kid living with parents. "Hey," I said one night, "Julie made those cookies for her Historical Society meeting."

Jimmy winked and whispered, "Then I'll just take two."

Even though Ipswich Lumber decided to keep my brother on through the year, he never offered a dime to help pay for groceries or rent. His excuse was saving for a house down payment.

Raking leaves on an October Sunday, I heard a battle cry from my past, "Anytime, anywhere!" and the bastard grabbed me from behind and wrestled me into a pile of leaves. I tried to roll him off–his jackal laugh hacked in my ears–but Jimmy pressed my face into the dank leaves. Just as suddenly, he released me. "Come on, Rog," he taunted, dancing a jig, "catch me if you can." I lunged for him, and he side-stepped me.

"You son of a bitch," I huffed as I ran after him–I felt a pain in that left leg.

"Careful what you say, lil' bro," he said as he hurdled the hedge; "we got the same mom."

I ripped a branch off a tree and lashed the air between us as I chased him. We were nine and thirteen again. Back on Sullivan Street. When a neighbor I didn't know drove by and honked, Jimmy returned a high-handed wave that could direct planes. It brought me to my senses. I dropped the stick and started inside, leaves in my hair and stuck to my sweater.

"Okay, Roger," he called, "I give. You win, bro."

*

When my bitching to Julie about Jimmy's smelly shoes under the living room coffee table unraveled a list of irritations, she reached both hands up over her head. "Loosen up, Roger! You have to go with the flow a little."

"Going with the flow is my brother's way," I snapped.

"Maybe you should try it. You could learn something from his free spirit."

"Free spirit my ass, free*load*er is more like it." I couldn't help but think that Julie found my brother attractive (the way she had laughed at his nudity in the hot tub, had invited him to stay, and had kept him working around her shop). With things like that night of painting together, was he slowly putting the moves on her, winning her as I lost her–a replay of Maggie twenty years later? Leaving for work to catch the 6:52 or 7:20 train to Boston and usually returning at 7:37 but often catching the 8:00 out of Boston, I provided ample time for Julie to be lonely and for Jimmy to woo my wife. I wanted to be more laid-back but felt forced, by Jimmy, into an excessively rigid posture if only as a juxtaposition to him, Jimmy the social and moral amoebae.

"He's a bottom feeder," I said. "I'm the responsible one, remember? That's how we ended up in a $900,000 house, and why you can dabble in antiques."

This "dabble" comment did not go over well and left me tailing Julie from the room apologizing. Meanwhile, my brother's rank shoes remained under the coffee table.

*

A week before Christmas, more than six months after his arrival, Jimmy came home excited. "Guess what, Roger?"

"You bought a house." I didn't even look up from *The Wall Street Journal*, didn't miss a beat.

"I bought a boat."

Now I crinkled the paper into my lap. "You did what?"

"A 14-foot sailboat. It's my Christmas present to the three of us. Remember the summer we learned to–"

"What is the matter with you?" I said. "Where's your down payment for a house?"

"Don't be such a boring old banker. Come on, bro, you got to have some fun."

"When are you going to grow up and be responsible?"

He gave me that grin and shrugged. "I am who I am."

That goddamn grin wouldn't get him out of trouble this time. I wanted to club him. I glared at my brother, determined to break his grin. But it wouldn't yield.

"So, when do you plan to buy a house, Skipper?" I asked, choking on my sarcasm.

"I don't know." He still grinned as he shrugged again and shook his head. "Probably never. It's a pipe dream, man. If you knew my credit–" He pawed the air. "Shit, man, I can't even get a *copper* MasterCard. Ain't no bank going to loan me money for a house."

My senses went dead under the weight of his words. My eyes searched for his laugh, searched for a sign that he was joking. "A pipe dream?" I muttered.

"You knew it from the start. I saw the doubt in your eye the first time I mentioned buying a house."

Another pipe dream like so many others. Tossing *The Wall Street Journal* on the oriental rug, I stood up (pain radiated from deep in my left thigh); part of me wanted to throw a roundhouse right into his face and fight out of the corner he'd pushed me into. I was not going to sit while he stood over me, was not going to yield the position of power. This was my space and, although this interloper had procured a foothold, I possessed the psychological advantage in my own living room. "When?" I rapped on the end table.

"When what?" He shrugged.

"When are you going to find a place of your own?"

"I don't know. Soon. I've looked at the papers, but the rents are high in this town."

As if questioning one of my direct reports in a job review about one of his professional goals–hands on my hips–I asked: "What's your timeline?"

He laughed. He laughed at me. "Timeline? Fuckin–a, Roger, not everybody plans and schedules their life. *Timeline*," he scoffed. "You probably schedule your daily crap."

(This was not true, but I usually went a little before ten o'clock in the morning, after my 9:30 cup of coffee, my second.)

"Do you plan to live with us forever?" I asked.

"I don't plan!"

"So you'll stay until I kick you out?"

"Are you kicking me out? It won't be the first time I felt the Membrook boot."

"Nobody ever kicked you out of the house."

"You little dumbshit. You think I wanted to take off after I broke your leg? I wanted to be with you, but the old man beat the living

shit out of me and said he'd kill me if I ever came back." I felt like I
was fourteen again. Jimmy looked at the ceiling and turned to the
window. "I bought that telescope to help you escape Dad and his
ways. After I bought it Mom talked the old man into letting me
come back. That telescope took every penny I had and everything
I could get for your bike too. But it worked. Look at you now."

I stood mute, looking at the wide pine floors of the living room,
the oriental rug, thinking of the telescope wrapped in silicone cloth
and packed away in the dark attic and how the instrument had
been the catalyst for my achievements.

"Guess I'll get my stuff and go," he said, turning from the room.

Where the hell was Julie? She could sweep in here and throw
herself on the conflict, smother it with womanhood and kindness.
But she was absent, so I had to say it. "No, stay. Stay, until we
can figure something out. Find you an affordable place." I felt the
muscles in my back tighten, as I postponed my goal to get rid of
my brother.

*

So we added a sailboat to our driveway. Actually, Jimmy parked
it on the dead grass beside the drive. His beater of a Chevy and a
pink ("It's not pink, Rog. It's faded red.") sailboat on a rusty trailer
sat outside our colonial-period home.

Although he never reported to me, he told Julie the apartments
he saw were either too expensive or a rat hole. With interest rates
falling, a mortgage payment for a small house, a fixer-upper, would
be less than rent and would be an investment. If only he could get
a mortgage.

And I could do it. Since I ran the mortgage department, I could
slip it through the system. He had, after all, rescued me with the
telescope that rocketed me out of the Membrook orbit. I didn't
want to do it. Strictly speaking, it was not illegal, but to handle

loans for friends or family cut against the Beacon Bank code of ethics. No matter what Jimmy had done for me, I still couldn't live with him. This way I could get rid of him and at the same time fulfill a past-due recompense. I owed the fathead, and I'd make good on my debt.

In January I house hunted for Jimmy and got Julie to help. Eventually she found a one-bedroom cottage, a box no larger than a standard two-car garage, just six blocks from us. It felt way too close—but then, the dark side of the moon would have felt too close. "In a town as small as Ipswich," Julie said, "he's a neighbor no matter where he lives." Or as Jimmy indelicately put it once: "When a mosquito farts on Crane's Beach, everyone in Ipswich smells it." The house had faded baby-blue aluminum siding, overgrown shrubs, stained ceilings from a leaky roof, and a musty smell. It was a dog. But it was a cheap little dog.

When I showed Jimmy the house, he said he wasn't sure this would work for him. Didn't think he could do a mortgage. What if he lost his job? What if he wanted to move?

"Here's the story," I said. "You can buy this house for a mortgage of about $450 a month and put some sweat equity into it, making it an investment. Or you can rent a place for twice the money with no investment or tax advantages. Or you can stay with us for one third of our mortgage payment which would be $1,500 a month—starting tomorrow." I gave him my version of his big grin. "So, what'll it be, bro?"

*

Greased by my authority, Jimmy's mortgage papers slid through the works in record time, and we closed on his house mid-March. Ten months after he arrived, he was out—my one and only New Year's resolution achieved.

*

Because New England banks remembered all too well swimming in foreclosed property in 2009–and Beacon Bank was no exception–the bank hired Ernst & Young to periodically audit mortgages to avoid risky borrowers. Since they'd done an audit the year before, I figured we were safe. If they did an audit that year, I hoped they'd somehow skim past Jimmy's mortgage, somehow not notice the bad credit rating or the two Membrook names. I hoped for the impossible.

One May afternoon, I was called upstairs to the boardroom which had a beautiful view high above Boston Harbor. But that day the blinds were drawn and at the far end of the room, a long, walnut table, set up like a dais, faced one folding metal chair in the middle of the room. A female voice over the intercom told me to be seated. I waited on the cold metal chair until Sumner Peabody, the bank's CEO; Emory Lambert, the president; Winthrop Bowdoin, executive vice president; and Peter Johns, chief counsel entered to take the four high–backed leather seats. I knew these men, we'd worked together for eleven years and had been on a first–name basis from the day I made VP, but these old boys of Boston now addressed me as if at a congressional hearing.

Sumner Peabody called the meeting to order and sat back.

Emory Lambert began: "Mr. Membrook, are you aware of the bank's policy against handling loan or mortgage applications for family or close friends?"

"I am." I tried to sit up straighter, but every time I leaned back, my butt kept slipping down on the slick metal seat.

"You knowingly violated that policy for your brother, James Membrook?"

"It was more of a circumvention." If I cushioned the crash, I thought I might escape with a reprimand. "As you know, it's not a crime. Which is not to say it wasn't wrong. But I was under a lot of stress. And that's the only time in eleven years with Beacon that I bent a rule."

"Please explain, Mr. Membrook, exactly why you handled your brother's application."

"He moved into our house, and he was driving me crazy." I laughed. They didn't. "I had to get him out, so I helped him get a mortgage, but he has–"

Sumner Peabody leaned in, "He was driving you crazy?"

"Not *crazy*, crazy. Just annoyed, highly annoyed. Like the night Julie and I were in the hot tub and he comes home all sweaty after a softball game and jumps in with us naked." I laughed again, but they didn't. "*We* weren't naked, Julie and me. My brother was naked." Not even a smile from them.

"What was the question again?" I asked.

"You answered it," Sumner said.

Now Winthrop waded in: "Have you handled mortgages for other friends or family?"

I sensed my career circling the drain. "Of course not. I take my job seriously and have for *eleven years*. I admit, I bent this one rule, one time. But my brother has a job, and he's making his payments."

"You know the bank is concerned about the stability of loans?"

"Yes, but his job–"

"Yet you approved a loan for your brother, who is clearly a bad credit risk?"

"Let's put this into perspective," I said.

"I think we've done that, Mr. Membrook," Sumner Peabody, the CEO replied. "Please wait outside."

"Hey, wait a minute. This is not the kind of thing I do. You guys know me. This is my first time taking a shortcut. And I've been good for this bank. I've made you guys a lot of money."

"Thank you, Mr. Membrook, please wait outside," Emory Lambert ordered.

"I wouldn't have written the mortgage unless I knew my brother could make his payments."

"Then why didn't you co-sign?" Winthrop asked.

Maybe I was crazy, but not *that* crazy, was my thought. I wanted to laugh at the preposterous idea that I'd put myself on the line for Jimmy's mortgage. But I said nothing.

"Please wait outside," Sumner said.

When they called me back in, not two minutes later, I didn't know if I should request a lawyer or a blindfold. The CEO and president were gone. Winthrop Bowdoin, the executive VP, a guy I considered a friend, had it all over his face, and his pulling the trigger with words was just a formality. And there it was: blam. As a banker, I was a dead man. The chief counsel never said a word.

As they left, Winthrop said, "Sorry, Roger."

"For one rule?" I asked.

"In an iffy economy, one rule is enough." He shrugged with open palms, and I could almost see a gold chain between his wrists. "One example goes a long way."

My guts rumbled as I got a black garbage bag and collected my things: bookends, a few books, rolodex, and a photo of Julie and me on the beach in Mexico. I studied my face in the photo, the Membrook resemblance. The eyes, the smile, the widow's peak–it was my father's face, my brother's, mine. Eleven years at the bank and all of my personal items didn't even fill one black garbage bag. Tossed my briefcase in there too. It was all garbage now. Behind my desk for the last time, I didn't want to leave. Everyone out there knew, and their eyes waited for me to open the door. I feared facing the hazel eyes of Debbie, my assistant, a timorous, junior-college dropout. Where would I go and what would happen to me after I opened the door? In shame, I lowered my forehead to the desk, the cool mahogany warming through the unblemished polyurethane. Recalling my former successes and stature at Beacon Bank, I remained tearless but longed for the release of weeping.

Then bang, the door flung open, clipping short my woolgathering. Debbie, a hand on the knob, a hand on her hip, "So, like, you ready to go, Mr. Membrook?" Her voice had a fresh snap to it that I'd never heard from her. "Ten minutes ago Mr. Bowdoin called. Told me to make sure you got your stuff, but no bank files or computer disks. And then to escort you out of the building. To make sure you didn't, like, steal or sabotage anything."

"I'd never do anything like that." I felt like I was speaking to a State Trooper who'd just pulled me over for speeding.

"That's what I said, but then he told me none of us knew you as well as we thought." She sorted through the garbage bag, pausing for a moment to apologize before opening my briefcase and extracting two files. Frozen and shamed by her audacity, I felt like a child. Had I fallen so fast and so far that even Debbie, with whom I'd had a good working relationship, could treat me this way? "Looks like you got everything. Ready to go?" Before I could answer, she said, "Oh, your stars." She lifted from the wall my map of the heavens. Originally I'd brought it to remind myself that I was not only a banker but also something of an astronomer and to remind me that Beacon Bank was not the only fixture in the universe. But it had long ago become a metaphor, at least for people around the office, of my career as a rising star.

"You can have it," I said. Then, "No, no, give it here." And I snatched it from her hands, cradling it under my arm. "Let's go."

I led the way, walking fast, meeting no one's eyes. Getting into the elevator and riding down the twenty-seven floors without speaking to Debbie. When the doors opened at the lobby, I strode out ahead of her and never looked back. I walked away from the towers of Boston's Financial District. Eleven years with Beacon and they'd ended it so easily, shooed me away like a stray mutt. Deep inside I felt a flicker of relief from the effort of trying to fit in with those bankers. Then it occurred for the first time that maybe I wasn't meant for banking, but on that day, I pushed the thought aside. If there were any financial jobs out there–and there weren't many–who would hire me?

At North Station, as I passed the fruit stand in the waiting room, my hand reached out and snatched an apple and pocketed it. What was I doing? Outside by the concrete platforms, I pulled the apple from my pocket, and my teeth snapped off a big sweet bite. I devoured the whole thing fast, taking huge bites so I couldn't close my mouth, juice dripping off my chin. When the train for Reading pulled out, I took a final bite and rifled the rest of it off the last car. A conductor at the next platform said something to me but turned away when my roaring laugh projected bits of chewed apple at him.

I wiped my mouth on my suit sleeve and sat on a bench to wait for the 3:15 to Ipswich. Accustomed to the throng of rush hour, I'd never looked at commuters, but with the small number of riders waiting, I studied them. A couple of mothers with shopping bags watched children play, a handful of college-age kids, a nurse in her white uniform, an old man with a bushy, gray mustache wore a Red Sox hat and read the *Boston Herald* sports page. One of the young mothers sat at the far end of my bench, holding a bag from The Museum of Science gift shop. We exchanged smiles and watched her two sons, probably six and four years old, repeat foot races between the columns on the platforms—watching their feet the way children do, unable to believe how fast the ground passes under them. I recalled Jimmy and me.

"These guys have worn me out today," she said.

"To have their energy," I responded.

She shook her head. "Oh, don't I know."

"And the rest of their lives are ahead of them," I added, feeling sorry for myself.

"We all have the rest of our lives ahead of us." She replied and smiled.

For a minute or two we said nothing but watched the boys playing tag. The younger one was "it" of course, and his frustration grew as he couldn't catch his older brother. Then the fuzzy public address system blared, "3:15 to Ipswich now boarding on Track 2," and the woman hurried to corral her boys.

A dizziness swirled as I watched her and the kids board the train. Not poor, but this was no six-figure income family, yet the woman's life looked rich to me right then. How much money did her family live on? How much could Julie and I manage on? I unbuttoned my collar and took off my tie, stuffing it into my black plastic bag with the rest of my professional life. I put the bag where the mother had sat and rested my head on it, closing my eyes. How easy it would have been to fall asleep and never go home, never explain to Julie, never have to blame Jimmy. Just fade away.

"3:15 for Ipswich departing Track 2," the speaker crackled. I opened my eyes and saw a young couple holding hands running to catch the train. The conductor granted them a smile, touching the bill of his cap before he waved to the engineer and stepped aboard. The train began to pull out, sliding through the chute of concrete platform, a pair of red lights glowing off the back above a gaping mouth. I leaped to my feet, sprinting down the platform, gaining on the train. Nearing the end of the platform, I reached the last door, and just before the conductor closed it, I sprang aboard. "Hi," I said, panting.

"Crazy," I heard the conductor mutter as I squeezed past him.

When I sat across the aisle and back one row from the mother and her two boys, she said hello, but I noted a touch of concern over my panting and my disheveled look. She handed each of her boys a rectangular box, which held small telescopes from the museum gift shop. The rest of the way, one eye squinted into a prune, they scanned the magnified world passing the train's window. Before they got off in Beverly, I handed my map of the galaxy to the woman. "I'd like to give this to your future astronomers, a map of the heavens," I said. "It's very educational." I felt like a salesman.

"Cool," the older boy said, standing on the seat for a look.

"Cool," the younger one echoed trying to see.

"It's a map of the night stars," I explained to the boys. "Stars have names and they can be mapped just like towns."

"Wow, really?" the older boy said. "Can we have it, Mom?"

"Yeah, can we, Mom?" the little guy followed.

"Okay," the mother said. "Thank you." And the boys thanked me too before she ushered them down the aisle and off the train.

*

When Julie got home from her antique shop, I stood in the kitchen, blue jeans, sweatshirt, sneakers. Four empty beer bottles lined up on the counter, a fifth in my hand.

"Hi. What are you doing home so early?" she said.

"Howdy, honey!" I replied, but I was not that drunk. Not yet.

"You okay?"

"I've had better days. I got fired this afternoon."

She hooked her hair behind her ear, and some of the color drained from her face as her blue eyes searched me for the sign of a joke. "You got laid off?" she mumbled.

"No, I got fired." And I tipped up the bottle for a nice big gulp.

"Fired?" Hands on the counter to stabilize herself.

"Yep, fired," I said. "Fired in cold blood."

"Oh, Roger," and she embraced me. "What happened?"

"Jimmy happened," I answered. "If it wasn't for him, I'd still have my job. His shitty little mortgage violated the bank's ethics policy."

She loosened her grip on me. "You broke the rules?"

"I had to or that bastard would've lived with us forever."

Julie embraced me again, but more like someone soothing an old dog. "How could they fire you after ten years for breaking one rule?"

"Eleven years. Today, one rule is enough. Enough for them to use you as a scapegoat and hold you up as an example so everyone toes the line."

"It was just one rule, right?" Her eyes shifted from one of my eyes to the other and back before I could catch up.

I broke her embrace and stepped back. "What? You think I'm like Jimmy? You think I cut corners and cheat?"

She stepped forward, her arms rising. "Roger, I didn't–"

I slapped her hands away, grabbed a couple of beers, and rushed out the back door. I jumped in my BMW but at the end of the driveway I didn't know which direction to go. Where did a guy with no job go? Then I saw Julie approaching in the rearview mirror. Left, a guy with no job went left. So I pulled out to screaming tires and, oh man, I almost got clobbered by a big Buick. So damn close a stolen apple core wouldn't have fit between us. The guy honked, and even though it was my fault, I rolled down the window and flipped him the bird.

Julie was screaming at me, but left, yes, left. To the beach. And I took off. My fingers tingled and my armpits itched from the near miss, so I leaned my head out the window like a hound to smell the fresh air and calm my nerves. I stayed out at the beach until dark, a night when clouds obscured the stars. My nerves were just beginning to fray.

Over the next six months, I scoured the Boston area for a financial job, draining my pool of contacts, which, as it turned out, were a mile wide but only an inch deep. I had a few polite interviews. But turned up zilch. Ended up taking an idiot job for six months at a little bank in Salem, Mass., working as a teller and consulting to their mortgage department for less than a quarter of my old salary. My greatest fear was that one of my old colleagues might see me tending the window. Now that I had to commute 25 minutes each way, I had a reason for the BMW, but I couldn't afford it and it was the first thing to go. Next, our house went on the market, but there weren't a lot of people eager to pony up $900,000 for the antique house, with its perpetual maintenance lists, and we took a terrible beating to unload it. We rented a condo in Ipswich until I could land a real job.

Around the first anniversary of getting fired from Beacon Bank,

Jimmy told me Ipswich Lumber planned to expand their operation and needed a Chief Financial Officer. My initial reaction was to pass, working at a lumber yard was one thing for my brother, another for me. The job paid less than half what I'd made at Beacon Bank, but about twice what I was making at the Salem bank, so I eventually looked into it.

When I showed up to interview in my Brooks Brothers suit, "Hey Jimmy, look at you," a big man in coveralls called, tromping across the lumber yard in worn and heavy work boots. "Thought it was your day off."

"I'm not Jimmy. I'm Roger Membrook, his brother," and held out my hand to shake.

"Bob Lane," his mitt of a hand swallowed mine, "glad to meet you. Boy, you sure look like Jimmy, but he ain't here."

"I'm here to interview for a job."

"Not a yard ape, like us. You're a banker or something, right?"

I nodded. "I'm here about the CFO job."

"A good word from Jimmy would help."

"That right?"

"Everybody likes Jimmy, especially Bill, the owner. Your brother ain't the best worker, but he gets it done and makes work fun for the rest of us. Boss calls him the Morale Czar."

Taking in the smell of sawdust and wood and sweat and dirt, something atavistic stirred in me. I could work here. I wanted to work here. The interview went well, and before going home, I stopped by Jimmy's to ask for a recommendation. A year earlier it would have seared me with shame to ask, but not now. My brother knew what it was to take a fall and promised to do all he could.

And, four years ago this week, I did get the job. Became Chief Financial Officer of Ipswich Lumber, thanks in part to my brother.

Do I miss the banker's life? Sure, at times. Friends in the financial world, who couldn't understand why I didn't fight to get back on the fast track, have slipped away. I miss the money and power of the old-boy's network. But I was never really a member.

Julie and I bought a simple frame house in a nice neighborhood, something like the place where she grew up. Eliminating two-plus hours of commuting and ten-hour work days, opened time to spend with Julie, and sixteen months ago, she gave birth to our first child, Michael Membrook. Now she's pregnant with our second. At 43, I'm an older father, but I have less stress and more energy for kids now than I ever had as a banker.

No more suits and ties to work either, just an occasional sports jacket. From my desk on the second floor, the guys of Ipswich Lumber tease me that I'm the paper man in a lumber yard. When it's slow in my office, I put on the coveralls that hang on the back of my door and go down to help Jimmy and the boys in the yard, feeling the weight of wood. At those times I can be a Membrook man—not my brother or my father, but a Membrook man just the same, a reality as undeniable as the movement of the planets.

Speaking of the planets, I also joined the North Shore Astronomers Club and became treasurer. I still use the telescope my brother gave me a long time ago. Seems I see out of it more clearly than ever.

This Boy's Game

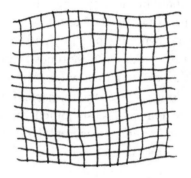

As deliberately as he had ever emerged from a dugout, Buddy "Slugger" Rogers stepped from his Jeep Cherokee and lumbered toward the factory gate, squeezing the sticky pine tar on his baseball bat.

The guard, a guy who'd played left field on the company team for a couple of years, scrambled from the glass booth. "Hey, Buddy. Ho, Buddy," his palms waving like paddles. "Can't let you in, Slugger."

"Outta the way," Buddy held off his ex-teammate with a stiff-arm and entered the executive parking lot, passing the "RCA Executives Only" sign without breaking stride. "Ain't gonna hurt nobody," he said. At the first oversized American car, he poked out the driver-side window with the bat, kind of cue-stick style. As the smell of leather seats reached him, he thought of the executive getting cold as he drove home that February night. By the fourth car, a Lexus SUV, Buddy was ramming the end of the bat through the glass and picturing an unsuspecting manager's head on the other side. Wham, right in the temple, bastard's skull shattering into little bits like the safety glass. By the time two factory security guards arrived–revolvers drawn–Buddy had both hands at the end of the bat swinging freely. Cubes of glass crunching under his feet as he stepped into his natural-looking swing to line-drive side mirrors off and spider-web windshields.

The guards, one tall and paunchy the other small and thin, eased Buddy's bat out of his hand and silently escorted him to his red, fourteen-year-old Jeep.

"Management figured something like this might happen," the tall guard said. "Damages will come out of your severance pay."

Buddy nodded. Then he said: "Them bastards, moving the whole friggin' thing to friggin', Mexico."

"It's a bitch, Buddy," the big guard said. Buddy didn't know the guards, but a lot of people at the plant knew Buddy Slugger Rogers. He was the best baseball player ever to suit up for RCA in the Indiana Industrial League. Nine times he'd made the I.I.L. all-star team.

"It ain't right," Buddy said, "moving Radio Corporation of *America* to Mexico."

"They've thrown us a curve, but what can you do when seventeen-year-olds down there work for thirty cents an hour and no benefits?" the big guard said.

Was that a whiff of whiskey Buddy smelled?

"These guys didn't make the decision anyway," the small guard said, chinning toward the management lot. "They're getting transferred or laid off too. Company headquarters is where you ought to bust a few windows."

"Maybe I will," Buddy said. "Where is it?"

"Hell, I'm not even sure," small guard said.

"Me neither," added old whiskey breath, "Indianapolis?" and the three of them shared a sardonic laugh and shook their heads.

"Pick up your bat tomorrow," said small guard.

"Keep it," Buddy tossed off and climbed into the Jeep. "Don't suppose I'll need the bat this spring." He started his truck then forced a laugh, "I went out with a bang, hey fellas? Batter up!"

The guards smiled, and the small one said, "Take it easy, Slugger. You'll get another job."

Roaring out of the lot, he rushed to get away from the factory as the shame of smashing up those cars came upon him. When he played ball, a determination, a hatred of losing, a concentrated rage rose in him like something brutal. Pitchers called him a mean son-of-a-bitch for his look that threatened and challenged. He never hesitated to take out a second baseman to prevent a double play or to blast a catcher who dared to block the plate. Off the field, he was a fairly easy-going guy. But something had snapped as he passed the gates of the executive parking lot and he reached in the back seat for his bat. What had it proved? He winced at the thought of himself smashing up those luxury cars and SUVs–side mirror cables jutting out like the veins of torn-off arms. Even in the moment, it had given him no satisfaction the way hitting a baseball always did. It had only served to blow most of his meager severance pay, probably all of it. What remained was embarrassment and the sweet smell of pine tar on his hands.

The pink slip burned in his shirt pocket. Another job? He didn't want no job. A man needed work, that was a fact, but his stupid job was just a job. It was the baseball he wanted.

He wondered if he could get a job at one of the other factories with a Division One Indiana Industrial League team. There were just two others in south-central Indiana. Westinghouse had frozen hiring a year ago, and at Cummins Engine in Columbus, UAW guys

cattled-up around the block for any job opening. So he wasn't
going to play for those teams.

Buddy had soldered wiring and computer chips on the RCA
assembly line for ten seasons, since he was nineteen, in exchange
for center field and clean-up in the batting order. And for money.
The paycheck meant more to Rhonda than Buddy.

Rhonda, he was in no hurry to see her, or the girls, so he decided
to drive back to Nema the long way, through Sycamore Springs
State Park. The radio said it was one o'clock and fifty-two degrees,
a warm and sunny February day, the kind of day that usually inspired thoughts of spring and baseball. Management had laid off
his production group at noon and gave them the afternoon off.
Didn't know what he'd do when he got home. Didn't know what
he'd do tomorrow. The Jeep slowed; shit, man . . . wouldn't see the
guys from his production group again, wouldn't see his old team-
mates. Wake up, have breakfast, and then what? Job hunt, open
the classifieds. He'd never really looked for a job before. He'd probably have to go to those career counseling sessions at the plant. All
of that started tomorrow morning–unemployment. The morning
would drag into a long afternoon, with Rhonda working in the
house doing the books for two shops in town.

Rhonda had worried about the layoffs. When he lied about
his production group manufacturing components for the Mexico
plant, he'd almost convinced himself. But knew she doubted his
words. So he was in no hurry to get home and tell her the truth.
Not now. Not yet.

Rumbling along the park's rutted gravel road, Buddy noted a
grove of hickories by their shaggy bark. It was his favorite tree. He
let the Jeep Cherokee roll to a stop and looked into the winter-gray
woods. Must be a million baseball bats in the hickories along this
road, he thought.

Then he told himself: They can take your job, Slugger, but
there's no way they can take your baseball. Pull yourself up by

your bootstraps. Don't get into a slump.

Right then, he decided to go pro like he should have eleven years ago. The Jeep started moving again. At twenty-nine, he'd be an old rookie at spring tryouts, but he was bigger, stronger, and smarter than when he got drafted out of high school. He really knew the game now.

If not for his father's death from a heart attack in the spring of Buddy's senior year and his mother's break down from it, he would've signed. But he had to get a job and carry the whole crew, kid brother and two little sisters. Couldn't let the younger ones quit school to get jobs. Even if he'd signed to play pro ball, back then farm teams barely paid prospects enough to live on. He had to stay. "Everything happens for a reason," became his mother's mantra when she sent him off to Nema Lumber Yard each morning. Buddy wasn't sure if she repeated it for him or for herself. Like a dog chasing a squirrel and getting choked at the end of his chain, Buddy almost caught his dream, and he had a hell of a time seeing any "reason" for his father's death or for killing his pro baseball career.

About the time tryout offers came the next spring, Rhonda got pregnant. So he married her. Buddy never regretted getting married to Rhonda, and from the day Kate was born, he never, ever regretted becoming a father. Not when Melanie came along three years later either. He and Rhonda had struck a deal before Kate was born—he got to name the girls and she got to name the boys. That's because he wanted to name a boy Mel and Rhonda hated that name for some reason. But that didn't stop him from naming his second daughter Melanie and calling her Mel all the time. And while he had to acknowledge a biased eye, those two little girls were the brightest and best looking kids in Nema, bar none. Kate and Mel, a pair of sprites, and they both loved baseball too.

After he and Rhonda got married, her old man got Buddy on at RCA in Bloomington. Good thing too, because Slugger's success in the Indiana Industrial League and the legend of Horace Hopper were the only things that kept him going to work. Years ago the Pirates pulled Horace Hopper out of the I.I.L, and he made a career out of bloop singles. That pud knocker couldn't carry Buddy's jock, and Old Horace made it. Half those candy asses up there today, crying about their millions, didn't have his stick, his arm, or his glove. "This boy's game is complete," a scout from the Reds had told Coach Sloan when Buddy was in high school. Then the scout put a stubby arm around Buddy, "You're the complete package, kid." That was eleven years ago. And he was better now, damn it. He was. If everything did happen for a reason, he'd prove it this spring.

In his excitement, Buddy drove faster on the gravel road, too fast. Pebbles clanging in the wheel wells. Buddy stretching a double into a triple. He burst over a rise and slammed into a wash-out. The Jeep was built for rough roads, but not that rough and not at that speed. Splashing in and bouncing over rocks he got to the other side. Now the steering wheel was cockeyed, and the Jeep nosed for the ditch. Totally whacked out of alignment.

Shit, there goes 90 bucks, Buddy thought. He slowed down but kept his excitement about going to spring training. Now he wanted to tell Rhonda.

"Hey, Rhonda," he cheered when he walked in, back-kicking the kitchen door to latch it as he slipped off his jacket. He paced through the house to find her at the dining room table and was irritated by the dread on her face.

"What?" he said.

"That's what I was going to say." She closed her bookkeeping. "Why're you home so early? You got laid off..."

"I got good news."

"Yeahhh?" she said warily.

"Yeah. I got laid off today—"

"Oh, no." Rhonda blanketed his chipper tone.

He felt anger rising, but reined it in and tried to recapture his optimism. "Hey, listen, Babe. There's a good part. Okay, here's the good part. I'm going to Florida for spring training." He punched his fist into his palm, into his imaginary glove. "I'm gonna play pro ball. There's nothing holding me back now."

He had never hit her pretty face (never hit her at all and never would), but this was the expression her face would take if he had. "Except a wife, two kids, and a mortgage," she said.

"After I catch on with a team, we'll rent an apartment in that city. We can keep this place for the off-season–lot of guys do that–or buy a big house over on Elm Street."

"What about school?"

"They got schools all over the country, Rhonda. Besides, most of the season is during summer vacation."

"What if you don't make a team?"

That was it. "Look," he said–suddenly his ear itched and he scratched it hard, digging his finger in as if he could pull that doubt out of his head–"what I need from you right now is support. I *can* do this. And I *will* do this. With you or without. Even if I got stuck in Double-A for a season, I'd pull down what I made at RCA."

"Buddy, I love you, and I know you love baseball–"

"More than anything."

That statement hung for a moment "–but it's a boys' game, and maybe it's time for you to give it up."

"I shoulda known I couldn't count on you. I shoulda known." Now he recalled all her bitching about how much time he gave baseball. Playing, and volunteer coaching at the high school, and going to games, and watching them on TV, and reading about baseball in the sports page or in magazines–Rhonda liked to call herself a baseball widow to friends. But his family never went hungry, and he took the girls along to games sometimes.

Once he'd tried to explain to her how he loved the drama of a game. No one knew the outcome until the end of the ninth inning–history in the making. That's what made sports the best entertainment (and baseball the best of sports because in football or basketball the outcome can be obvious in the last minutes). Better than movies where *somebody* knew the ending, even if it was only the creators. Buddy felt duped by that. Rhonda hadn't understood.

He'd slow cooked another speech over years, and he finally took the lid off. "Here's how it is," he rolled his weight from one foot to another like he did in the batter's box before the pitch came in, "baseball is what I do and is what I am. Like a doctor is a doctor, a first–class baseball player is a baseball player. He might be other things too, a husband, a father, even a lousy factory worker, but he is a baseball player first. You knew I was a baseball player before you married me." He paused for a second to consider if he wanted to ... to burn off this whole field, but sometimes you have to burn off a field before you can plow and replant. "To be first class–at anything–you got to make sacrifices, and I want to be a first-class baseball player. If something gets in the way," he pointed at her, "it gets shoved aside. Got it?"

"Oh, I got it all right," she said through tears of fury. She stood up to face him. "You're so full of horse shit, Buddy, your eyes are brown. You don't think I've made sacrifices? Now listen up, Pete Rose." She was the one pointing now. "I'm a first–class parent. And you know what it means to be a first-class mom in a family where the father puts baseball first? It's like being a single parent for six months. Actually year-round, because even when you're here, you're not here. You're mentally off chasing a pop fly or swinging your bat. I have to work twice as hard to keep the family together. That's my sacrifice."

God–damn he loved her. How could you help but love that no-shit personality? If the world had half her spunk, he thought, it would be twice as interesting.

"They're blue," he said, feeling himself grin.

"What!?"

"My eyes." He fluttered them at her, dipping his chin to his shoulder.

"Don't get cute, Buddy. I'm good and mad. I hardly ever complain about your love for this boys' game. When we were first married and the girls were little, you talked about going down for spring training, and I never objected. But you never went. Why not? In all these years, I never said you couldn't play, or coach, or watch. I figured you'd outgrow it. Now I want to know when. When will you outgrow it?" She took a breath and let that hang in the air.

Then she said: "You always say, everything happens for a reason." She was right, he had picked that up from his mother. "Maybe the reason you got laid off is that it's time to quit baseball."

"You got it wrong," he insisted. "It's the other way around. The reason is so I can play pro ball before it's too late."

"Why didn't you go before? When we just had Kate or before the girls were in school?"

He didn't answer. He didn't know the answer.

Now it was her turn to pause, and he wondered what was coming. Then she wound up and delivered, "Honey, you know you never really learned to hit a good curve. What do you think Major League pitchers would do to you?"

Now she was throwing at his head, a cheap shot. "You never believed in me, but I'll show you." He rushed, almost sprinted, out of the house.

"I'll show everybody," he muttered as he got in his Jeep. Down the drive, but not fast. The weight of his talk with Rhonda was already taking hold, his ear itching again. Besides, he had to wrestle the wheel to keep the Jeep out of the ditch. As he realized what an ass he'd been to his wife, the anger flowed out of him. He regretted the bullshit threat in his: 'if something gets in the way, it gets shoved aside.' She was right. He'd given too much to the game. Now it was his chance to make all that he'd given pay off, to collect as a pro. Yes, he'd have to give up baseball someday. But not yet. He was only twenty-nine, and the bigs were full of guys in their thirties. Some were forty. Still, shoulda kept his big mouth shut, hitting her with the lay-off and then leaving for spring training. Stupid. He'd have to apologize. When he did, he knew she wouldn't blow it out of proportion and kick his ass with it. That wasn't her way, and it was one reason he loved her so much. She wouldn't take his crap, but she could take being wronged. The woman had backbone, and he loved her for it. If it weren't for Rhonda's strength and her competence with the girls, he wouldn't be able to head for Florida. She could keep the family together until he caught on with a team.

Provided he *could* catch on with one.

And he could.

Without thinking, he'd driven to Sassafras County High School. Might as well go in and take some batting practice.

Slugger interrupted the quiet of Coach Sloan's study hall. "Hey, Coach," Buddy whispered from the door.

Coach Sloan looked at him like 'What the hell are you doing here? It's the middle of the school day,' but he motioned Slugger in. "What's wrong?"

"Nothin'. Just wanted to borrow your keys to the gym," Buddy said. "Gonna take a little batting practice." Sloan handed him the keys and ordered a couple of kids in the back of the room to be quiet.

Down at the gym, Slugger turned on the lights in the corner over the batting cage that he and Coach Sloan had built of two-by-sixes and white nylon netting. He was soothed by the gym's smell of sweat, leather, and rubber. With the gym quiet as a chapel, and with the rest of it in darkness, the batting cage at the far end looked like an altar.

Slugger took a bat from the cardboard barrel, examined it end to end, shook it by the grip, then dropped it back into the barrel with a drum–like thud. Too bad he didn't have his bat. Then he checked another and another until he found a decent fit. When he took the hickory in his hands, it felt like an extension of his arms. A born hitter people had always said of him, a natural. And at twenty–nine, he'd gotten better.

He ducked into the batting cage and loaded a bag of balls into the Iron Mike and set it on high. The first ball rattled down into the pitching machine and the metal arm circled around and hurled the white sphere toward Slugger. "Crack," it shot off his bat into the nylon netting. It felt good to hit the ball. It felt right. He could imagine Jessie and Mel cheering for him. Then, between each pitch, Slugger imagined himself playing for a different major league team, and he mumbled the team name: "Cubs," crack, into the ivy at Wrigley Field. "Pirates," crack, grounded into the hole at Three Rivers. "Red Sox," crack, lined off the Green Monster. "Reds," crack into the upper deck at Riverfront. Slugger smacked each ball the shaky old Iron Mike could throw at him.

He picked up the balls scattered around the cage to reload the machine.

What if he couldn't make a team, even a Double-A club? What would everyone in Nema think? And all the guys he'd played with over the years? Everyone thought he could be one of the players on TV. They all said so. Kids in Nema even took his name as often as big leaguers when playing sandlot games. But what did they know? None of them knew a major league player. People in town lamented how the fate of a fallen father, a weak mother, and a forced marriage had conspired to keep their star from shining before millions. Was it true? What if he went to spring training and proved them all wrong by failing to make a team? He'd never been cut. How could he come home and be who he was–the one who could have been?

Is that why he'd never tried before?

Before the machine hurled the next pitch Buddy Rogers stepped somewhat apart from himself and saw himself, a twenty-nine-year-old man in the corner of a high school gymnasium rapping baseballs thrown from an aging Iron Mike. A ball rattled down into place and the arm came around to deliver. The pitch curved toward him, he swung, and he missed it.

Twice Too Young

"No," the lovely, young woman whispered with weak conviction.

Linda held her 17–year–old daughter's hands across the corner of the marbleized Formica table. "Melanie," she said, "these days a girl doesn't have to go through with it. When it happened to me, I didn't know about such things, and it was illegal. But you're a smart girl. You could go to college, get out of here, become something."

"No," Melanie answered.

"Have you thought about life with John? He'll lose his Butler football scholarship and stay here. You know I love that boy, but men who end up here, often end up like your father."

"He was good enough for you."

Linda took a deep breath. "I made the best of the last 17 years with him and you kids. But, Melanie, honey, I had big dreams." Linda remembered how ashamed she had felt when she told the principal why she had to leave school. It was harder than telling her parents. He had put a large hand on her small shoulder when she began to cry, and said some child would be very lucky.

"But it's wrong," Melanie said.

"Is it right for a girl like you to be trapped in a town like this? Or a boy like John?" Linda asked. "Which is more wrong, Melanie June? Which is more wrong?" And when the 17-year-old girl lifted her face, she and Linda, both with oak-color hair and slate-blue eyes, looked more like sisters than mother and daughter with just 17 years between them. "If you love him, if you love yourself," Linda said, "give yourselves a chance to grow. There will be a time for this thing."

Linda remembered so well over a quiet moment the course of her days, and she wanted to shield Melanie from the oxymorons of her life: the crowded loneliness, the screaming silence, and the sullen joy. These Linda had known for half her 34-years but could not articulate.

"I'll finish high school," Melanie said, no doubt remembering her parents fighting over her mother wanting to attend night school to get her high school diploma. Her father had accused her mother of trying to prove she was better than he was.

"I'd like to see you finish college. You could be the first on either side of our family to graduate college," Linda said.

That thought hung between them for a moment, and then Linda told Melanie that ten years after she'd dropped out, when Tony had started trucking for McLean and all three kids were finally in school (Melanie in fifth grade, Mike in fourth, and Susie in first), Linda had made a trip to Bloomington. She'd planned to enroll in correspondence courses for her high school degree through the university. After signing up, she followed some students into an

ivy-covered limestone building, Woodburn Hall, and sat in the
back of a theater-like classroom with about a hundred students.
A small energetic man with gray curly hair talked about volca-
noes. It was fascinating. So she bought the textbook, and every
Tuesday and Thursday that semester, she went to his class. She
read the books when Tony was on the road. After Geology, she'd
sat in on Art History, then Political Science, Literature, Biology, and
so on at the rate of one course per semester over the past seven
years. While the rest of her life conspired to make her old, among
the students she felt young. But at times she stopped and looked
at them, realizing how much older she was now. One of her professors had been younger than she was, and she thought maybe
it was time to stop sneaking into lectures, but she wondered what
she would do with herself. Those classes had gotten her through
the week, every school week for years.

Linda said she just knew Melanie would love college if she went.

The fragile conversation between mother and daughter shat-
tered when Mike and a friend charged in through the kitchen door
from playing basketball in the gravel driveway. Linda tried to send
them out, but they wanted a drink. "Use the hose," she ordered, and
Mike knew by Mom's voice and Melanie's downturned face not to
argue. But he didn't display any worry either, and ran out the back
door with his buddy.

"If you'd had the choice, Mom, would you have done it?"

"That's not what we're talking about."

"It's what I'm asking," Melanie said.

"Melanie, I love you. From the moment I saw you, you were the
most beautiful thing I'd ever seen, and I never regretted a thing.
But we're talking about you, Melanie June. There's a big world
outside Nema, Indiana, a different world than I grew up in, and a
bright girl like you can make it your own."

"It ain't right, Momma."

"No it *isn't*. Both are wrong," Linda said. "You have two bad choices."

"Two wrongs don't make a right."

"Unless the second rights the first." Linda answered softly but firmly and stroked her daughter's hair. "This thing would change you and John forever. It would rob your youth. You'd have to scrape for everything. You'd be trapped. This thing would make you row far from the shore. I know, I've lived it before you," she said. "You have seen me live it."

"But John is different than Dad."

"Tony was a lot like John when he was 18. And John might end up a lot like Tony when he is 35. *Unless*, unless he gets an education and gets out of here." Linda pointed to the Lazy Boy in the living room. "Your father leaves his best self out on the road. When he's here, he's sitting in that recliner with a beer in one hand and the TV remote in the other, not talking unless he has to, and not looking away from the screen when he does talk, saving money for a bigger cable-TV package instead of a trip to Europe."

Melanie picked at the nail polish on her fingers, "What about me. If I stay, will I end up like you?"

"You might. Or like your father's sister, Beverly, whose dreams never reach far from their mobile home. But you don't want to live like either of us. You don't have to, Honey."

Melanie's hand rested on her jeans between her hip bones. Her hand slid down over the bump and four fingers held herself where it was soft. And she bent forward on the table resting her forehead on her other arm. When Linda's hand stroked the oak-colored hair again, Melanie began to weep.

Linda spoke softly because she could speak no other way with her throat so tight, "My sweet baby, sweet Melanie. There will be a time for this. But you can only be young and free once." She whispered as she rubbed her daughter's back and stroked her hair: "Fill your life with all the wonderful things." Linda felt her lovely girl nod under her hand. "My baby, my beautiful baby." Linda's finger expertly lifted a tear from the corner of her own eye before it could roll onto her cheek. Before it could be called crying.

An Imperfect Union

Finally it was my turn for adventure. In the spring of 1969, my parents were taking the family to the mythic land of Florida and my first trip out of Indiana. My three older siblings had visited Florida for spring break with friends, and many of my classmates had gone with their families. All returned with bronzed skin and tales of summer weather in March, vast beaches, and salty seawater. Treasures came north in the form of seashells that put to shame the coin-sized shells I pulled from Mud Creek–and some of my friends brought back little stuffed alligators. Real alligators, which perched on bedroom bookshelves.

We were going to stay with my grandparents, who wintered in St. Petersburg, renting a pastel-pink cottage with mint-green seahorse shutters on a bay. Each February they sent a big white box from the Sunshine State for my brother's birthday, a case of oranges like a summer miracle to shatter the depth of winter. Those sweet orbs with the squirt of juice tasted of magic, of Florida.

A week before the trip, a 26-foot cabin cruiser appeared in our gravel driveway. The boat's turquoise and pink fiberglass and round-shoulder styling said 1950s as clearly as its faded, chalky surface, and grayed wood trim spoke neglect. This promised to double the adventure in my mind. But my parents sparred over the craft. Mom argued to leave it behind, but my 18-year-old brother and I rallied behind the old man on this one, and Mom caved. All that week before we left, Dad worked on the old Johnson outboard motor, its cover on the floor of the garage like an oversized football helmet. He also replaced trailer tires, rewired tail lights, and rebuilt the rusted winch.

Then, the night before we left, my father got a phone call. When he hung up an energy radiated from him. "Come on, Matt," he said to me–his boyhood Tennessee accent surfacing as it did when he was happy or angry. He suppressed a giggle like a kid about to ambush a buddy with a water balloon.

"Where we going?"

"Come on, come on, come on," he bubbled, "you'll see when we get there."

We got into the family car–another of the former wrecks he had rebuilt in the garage. He tapped a beat on the steering wheel, reflected on cruising around the Gulf of Mexico in the boat, and chattered about taking me on a private deep-sea fishing trip.

A Volkswagen Beetle with peace signs painted on the doors and anti-war bumper stickers cut us off. My father blasted the horn and skidded to a stop alongside it at the next stoplight. He rolled down the window, and heaved his large head and upper torso out to holler and shake his fist at the offender, calling him a draft dodger and yelling, "America Love It or Leave It." At that, the peacenik in the Volkswagen ran the red light to make a sudden left turn to get away. My old man hooted and pounded the steering wheel, "Guess I spooked the little hippie."

We drove to a used car lot, and Dad told me to wait in the car. He reached under his seat and pulled out a battered paper bag, about the size of lunch bag.

A tall, thin man greeted him with a big handshake, and Dad handed him the bag. The man glanced around before taking it. They went inside the small office, which looked like a former gas station.

When Dad came back, he said: "Come on, Matt, we're taking another car home."

I followed him past a row of gleaming cars, hoods reflecting the strings of naked light bulbs and flickering plastic pennants, until he stopped at a long, gray Cadillac Fleetwood. "Whadaya think?" He glowed with the air of a lottery winner. How could I say I was horrified at the idea of riding in a rich man's car, a gas-guzzling environmental disaster? Then I imagined my mother's response; how could I say it was cool? Even at twelve years old, I knew of my family's tight money. And my brother, Chris, a senior in high school, had made the whole family well aware of his anti-war, anti-establishment political awakening. My sisters too, who were both at college and were catching the bus to meet us in Indianapolis, were likely to disapprove. I could already hear them. No, this car was not good. But I never had to answer because the old man was on a jag.

"We're riding to Florida in style!"

I opened the heavy door and looked at those huge bench seats, stretching out like a pair of sofas, and slid in next to my father. He drove it hard, chortling about Caddy's power and pick up as its hulking body rolled, yacht-like, through turns. He was having a ball—and I half-expected him to break into song with "Good Ol' Rocky Top" as he sometimes did—until I timidly asked if we could afford to buy this car.

"I didn't buy it. I called in a favor so we can use it for a week." Buoyant again, he added, "With this baby, we won't even feel that boat behind us, and there's plenty of room for all six of us. Just wait until your mom sees this."

I couldn't imagine her being happy about it. Despite my old man's bulk and bluster, it was my mother who was the strength in the family. And when the Caddy splashed into our gravel driveway, I knew they were headed for a showdown. He honked a few times and called her to come out and see. Then he stood in front of the Caddy like a proud child. But her hard, Chicago-accent popped his balloon.

"What is *that?*"

"Our ride to Florida."

"Oh, no it's not," she said. "You take that thing back where you got it."

My father, baffled by her response, said, "I won't."

"Yes you will, Dale." Her voice, though not loud, carried a burning intensity.

At that point I retreated to the bedroom my brother and I shared. Lurking near the door, I listened to my father's voice slide into a whining tone, claiming it was too late to take the Fleetwood back. Because he'd taken our car in to have work done on it. And he couldn't get it back if he wanted to. And he didn't want to and so on. He claimed the Cadillac hadn't cost us a dime but was loaned in return for a favor. Just like the boat, he explained. (Until then, I'd thought the boat was ours to keep.)

When Chris got home, he blew a gasket. His anti-establishment attitude included anti-materialism, anti-capitalism and anti-displays of wealth. And nothing said Rich Establishment like a Cadillac Fleetwood.

When tempers had flared over the Vietnam War, my father in favor, my brother against, of course, Mom never said anything.

She'd let the arguments last a little, and then she'd wade in and put a stop to it, saying: "Okay, that's enough you two. We're not going to settle it tonight." Chris usually retreated to our bedroom, slamming the door. Then he'd launch into a diatribe about how our parents were drunk on patriotism and blind to the evil of the war and the US military. But Mom never took sides, and she always came into our room to smooth Chris's feathers. My sense was that she was against the war but she had to keep the peace with our father.

About the Cadillac, Chris ranted to me with the force of a fighter: "I'm not going if we're going in that rich man's piece of shit. They can fucking forget it."

But to my father Chris's tone spun out as more of a whimper, "I don't want to ride in that fat-cat car. Come on, Dad, do we really have to take it?"

Now it was Big Dale's turn: "That's enough out of you. Just shut up. We're taking that car, all of us, and that's the end of it." My father's booming voice evoked visions of cocked elbows, closed hands, that expressed a clear and real subtext of violence.

All discussion about the Fleetwood ended.

The house remained eerily quiet the rest of the night but an energy hung in the air that threatened, at any moment, to generate a bolt of lightning. Chris stormed into our bedroom, hissing his rage and pummeling his pillow. This really screwed up his plan to drive to Sarasota to meet one of his buddies vacationing with his family. How could he hope to score some cool girls driving *that* car?

*

Early the next morning, we loaded bags into the Fleetwood's cavernous trunk and hit the road. Chris slept across the back seat so I rode between my parents–slowly cooking in the heat of anger still flowing between them–to the Indianapolis bus station to pick up my sisters.

At the bus station, my mother told us to stay in the car, and she'd find my sisters. No doubt she warned them not to talk about the car or the boat. But we heard them coming–Patty and Jo were laughing at the ridiculous sight of us in the rich man's car with the poor man's yacht. My mother tried to stifle them to no effect. My father got out and yelled at the three of them: "Not a word. Not one word." Instead of packing my sisters' bags in the trunk which had plenty of room, Dad simply heaved their bags into the boat.

First Patty and then Jo kissed their hands and reached into the car to pat me on the head and tousle my hair with a laugh.

"Love you, Matty." And "Love you, little brother."

"Love you guys too," I said. And I did love them–these two beautiful girls who brought a jolt of positive energy. More than sisters they were best friends and helped each other re–direct anger, embarrassment, and frustration, to laugh at most everything, mustering a what–the–hell–we're–in–the–soup humor to the crazy.

I'd seen this kind of friendship between my mother and her friend Jean from Chicago. Dad never liked Jean much, so we only saw her about once a year. But I loved it when Jean was around, she made my mom laugh and laugh. They'd sit at the kitchen table and drink coffee and talk until noon. Then they'd go out to dinner together and come in late laughing and whispering. When she visited last summer, I was eavesdropping when they talked about their kids. Jean went on about her two sons at Oak Park High School. After they went on and on about everyone else, Jean finally asked: "Ellen, so what about Matty? How's Matt?"

"Oh, Matt is Matt," my mother said. "He'll be fine. I wish he did better in school, but he just seems to roll along, pretty happy kid. I don't worry too much about Matt."

And that was it.

Was I fine? Was I just rolling along?

Outside the Caddy, my sisters quibbled briefly over who sat in the middle of the seat before settling it with a quick game of rock-paper-scissors. Jo lost and slid in next to Chris with a nudge and a kiss on the head. My brother groaned and yielded some room. At over six feet tall and with a history of car sickness, Chris always got the seat behind my mother. I got stuck between my parents when the six of us went anywhere, but I was now bigger and taller than my mother, nearly as tall as my sisters; yet I was still wedged between Mom and Dad. Somehow this felt like my reality: with my siblings nine, eight, and six years older—it was *them* and *me*. They did the important things, and I tagged along. Just rolling along, as my mom had said. My sisters whispered and snickered in the back seat as Dad fired up the giant V-8 engine.

He clicked on the radio to a Muzak station, playing a de-flavorized orchestration of The Beatles' "Sergeant Pepper's Lonely Hearts Club Band."

"Let's all be quiet and listen to some music," Dad said and turned it up loud.

Chris muttered: "You call this music?" Patty and Jo laughed.

"ENOUGH!" That accent again, followed by a hard blow to the steering wheel, serving as a shot across the bow.

Mom glanced at me and cocked an eyebrow, her lips going flat.

The car went quiet, except for the Muzak oozing from the speakers. Dad glared into the rearview mirror, stretching his neck to look into the back seat. Then our helmsman refocused, steered out of the parking lot, and we hit the road.

My father's plan was to drive the 1,000 miles from Indianapolis to his parents' cottage in St. Petersburg straight through, saving the cost of a motel. But somewhere in Alabama, he got off track trying to take a shortcut intended to, "Leave all those idiots stuck in bumper-to-bumper interstate traffic," and his long-haul plan ended up as hopelessly lost as we were. Everyone struggled not to say anything, Patty and Jo whispering and tamping down laughter.

Chris mostly remained in a Dramamine-induced coma. I crossed my arms, trying to keep from touching either parent in fear of a scalding.

Finally my mother blurted out, "I can't believe this! How did we get this lost?!"

"You shut your damn mouth," Dad shot back. "I don't want to hear a word out of you or anyone else," Dad said jabbing a finger at my mother across my face and then glaring in the rearview mirror.

"We have to stop at a motel," my mother said, her Chicago vowels unequivocal. "We are not going to drive all night."

"Okay. All right," my father barked in retaliation.

It felt like these volleys shot back and forth right through my head.

This would mark my first stay in a motel or hotel, and I wanted to be excited, but everything felt weirdly dangerous. Then one motel after another was full. Finally, a pathetically feeble little rainbow of neon had "vac-n-y" glowing below. When my father went inside to see about a room, Jo whispered, "Let's hope it's full," and we all burst out laughing to shatter the tension. But when Dad emerged from the office dangling a room key, we buttoned up. He'd taken the last room. There was a good reason The Rainbow Motor Lodge was the only place with a vacancy. White paint chipped off the low-slung, concrete-block building. The swimming pool was empty but for a swirl of black-green water alive with croaking frogs. The room was musty, carpet stained, and the yellowed ceiling was missing a couple of tiles. Then I had to sleep in Mom and Dad's bed, squeezed in next to my mom. Chris got the last cot. My minimal enthusiasm for a hotel stay went down the drain faster than water in the rust-stained toilet.

*

The next morning, my father, hunched over maps with a cigarette dangling from his lips, plotted a sure-fire shortcut to slash at least two hours off of our trip, cutting off those stupid southbound Yankees married to federal interstates. Next thing we knew we were back in that car, the pride of GM, barreling down another unlined, Alabama highway which could pass for a wide country road, slashing through miles of wilderness and bifurcating cotton fields.

We passed shacks of tar-paper, scrap wood, and corrugated metal, with junk cars and outhouses in the grassless yards of red clay. I couldn't believe people still lived like that in a country that put a man on the Moon. At one cluster of four shacks, skinny, half-dressed black kids and bony dogs lingered around the red-dirt yards. Three miles down the road at another cluster of similar shacks, we saw under-fed, half-dressed white kids and more mal-nourished mutts. At both places, grayed underwear hung out on the line for all to see.

We watched these shacks as we blew by, and none of us said a word.

The sight of these desperately poor people made me feel rich, made me feel sorry for the disparity between them and me, made me angry when I thought of really rich people. I wondered if those poor people hated us as we powered past them in the rich man's car.

Every small southern town we passed through seemed to have a limestone statue of a Confederate soldier with his back to the north. Confederate flags were commonplace, and bumper stick-ers boasted, "The South Will Rise Again." Worse than feeling like a foreign country, it felt hostile toward northerners.

My old man tore down the road as it undulated through miles of marshy wilderness, my stomach and testicles feeling a lift as we crested each hump in the highway. Suddenly, bam, bamble-bam-bam-bam. My father swearing as he wrestled the steering wheel and stopped the Fleetwood in the sandy shoulder.

The boat trailer had lost a wheel leaving the hub mangled.

There we sat in the middle of nowhere. We hadn't even seen one of those shacks or passed a single car since any of us could remember, let alone a service station. Patty and Jo didn't laugh at this mess.

My father ordered the four of us kids to find that wheel while he inspected the damage. He had to unpack the trunk to get the jack out and lift up the trailer to check the damage. It was 85 degrees under a blistering sun, and the humidity around that swamp made the sky a hazy white, like Indiana in August. Our clothes went damp just standing around. Chris and I went up one side the road, Patty and Jo on the other side. We'd wagered a Florida milkshake over which team would find the wheel first, boys vs girls. We waded through knee-high grass that sloped down from the elevated highway. A six-foot-long bull snake slithered through the grass ahead of me. Back home, I might have tried to grab it, but with thoughts of cottonmouths, my knees went wobbly. I looked off into the swamp thinking the wheel could be sinking in muck out there among the water moccasins. We searched down past the first gouge in the road where the wheel came off. Nothing. We called back our report.

"Just FIND IT!" our father screamed.

Suddenly a few water moccasins didn't seem so bad.

We re-jiggered the teams, Patty and I took one side, Chris and Jo the other as we worked our way back. The wager remained–now it was middle kids vs oldest and youngest.

Seconds later, we heard the big V-8 rev and tires spinning as the Fleetwood fishtailed onto the highway, leaving our mother standing in a cloud of dust beside the cockeyed boat. She watched down the road, hands on hips until the car was out of sight.

Then she turned on a heel and walked toward us, a white-hot anger locked in her jaw. She said we had to find the stupid wheel, and we went at it with renewed rigor. We weren't going to let her down. Three times we combed the high grass, walking into the spongy, muddy woods. This whole ordeal–the boat, the trailer, the

Fleetwood, the getting lost–all of it was my father's fiasco.

Finally, Patty and I spotted the wheel–at the same time. Actually, I thought I saw it first. She said she saw it first. But we each claimed to have found it. Then Patty, my ever loving sister, grabbed my t-shirt and got right up in my face. I thought she was going to punch me in the nose. "I found it Matty, so shut the fuck up."

"Patty!" My mom said.

"WHAT?"

"Don't talk like that."

"Oh, Mom, give it a rest. Matt has heard that word at school every day since second grade."

Patty still gripping my shirt, turned and shoved me. "Now help me get that stupid wheel out of the mud, Matt, so we can get the hell out of here."

Chris came over and volunteered to help me pull the wheel from the muddy swamp–water so Patty wouldn't ruin her shoes. We got pretty muddy, but we got the damn wheel, and we rolled it down the road.

Mom sat alone in the shade of the boat at the edge of the road. She looked off into the distance as if she were alone.

Patty and Jo had walked up the road a piece and talked quietly. Pretty soon they were laughing and turned around to come back.

I sat next to Mom and Chris a few feet away. Patty walked up and sat next to me. "Hey, kiddo, sorry I blew up at you," she said. "It wasn't about you."

"I know," I said but wanted to ask what it *was* about. "It's okay," I said.

"No, it's not okay," Mom stated without breaking her stare into the swamp.

"Mom," Jo said sitting next to Mom and putting a hand on her arm, "yeah, it kind of is."

And Mom let it go.

Then the five of us sat quietly in the shade of the boat, waiting for Dad to return. God it was hot. A few cars passed by. A pickup stopped to offer help, the driver ogling my mother and sisters before going on.

Simmering in the slow steam of Alabama, waiting for Dad, I'm sure we all wondered down deep if the old man would never come back for us. Deeper still, we all probably wondered if we might not be better off if he didn't.

Eventually he did return. It took more than an hour to replace the hub, get the wheel on, and hit the road. We reached my grandparents' house in St. Petersburg after midnight. There wasn't room for all of us in the two-bedroom cottage, so my sisters slept in the screened-in porch; Chris and I slept in the boat parked in the driveway. The boat's low cabin was cozy with two curved couches/beds along the hull, room for us in sleeping bags. Despite the musty smell and the broken-down pads, I thought the cabin was cool, like a cave or a tent. And we could peer out through oval portholes about the size of a hand.

*

On the first morning of vacation, while Dad left with the Fleetwood and the boat, Mom walked us four kids to the beach–about a mile away. Mom and I marveled at the palm trees and the lush green plantings everywhere. My siblings had seen all of this before on their trips to Florida with their friends' families, but Mom and I were rookies. She loved the exotic flowers. Then we saw the sand. It was as white as our northern skin, and we paused a few yards onto the beach to marvel at how it stretched for miles in both directions.

"Last one in's a rotten egg," Mom shouted, already in a full sprint. The rest of us yelled and tossed aside beach gear to chase after her. Chris veered over and gave me a shove, sending me sprawling in the soft sand. I rolled to my feet and ran after them. Chris dove into the first wave, and I ran smack into it only to get knocked on my butt, for my first taste of saltwater peppered with a little sand.

We played in the waves together most of the day, pausing for a lunch of hotdogs and ice cream from beach vendors. Patty and Jo goofed off and splashed and initiated the building of a sand castle like a couple of little kids. It was the most fun I could remember the family ever having. Eventually we walked back to my grandparents' cottage. Chris and I fished from their dock and caught crabs with long-handled nets. At some point, a subtle but unbending warmth came upon our beach-going gang, that oh-no of sunburn for underestimating the merciless Florida sun.

No one had heard from Dad all day until near dinner when he chugged up in the cabin cruiser (minus the outboard engine cover which was on the floor of the boat) and tied up at our grandparents' dock to our cheers. When he cut the smoking engine, it rattled, clamored, and coughed one more gasp of blue-white smoke before dying with a metallic clank. He eyed the engine before turning back to his family and stepped onto the dock with arms raised in victory, our smiling hero. We cheered again.

"Can we go for a ride, Dad?"

"Yeah, let's go."

"Come on, everybody, Dad's gonna take us out in the boat."

"Hold on," my father hollered over us. "Maybe after dinner. I have to do a little work on the engine yet. She's running pretty rough."

After dinner, he was back out in the boat messing with the engine. As had so often happened at home, I got stuck holding the flashlight.

"Hey, hey, pay attention," he said. "Right here. You see where I want the beam of light?" I adjusted the flashlight. "Good, now don't move, damn it."

It was deadly dull, holding a flashlight for him. He seldom told me what he was doing but muttered to himself a good deal, often hurting a finger and spinning a rope of curses under his breath.

"What?" I'd ask.

"Nothing! I'm just thinking out loud." And a few seconds later, he'd bark, "Hey, did you hear me? I said hand me the half-inch socket. Pay attention, Son."

Of course my mind wandered. Sitting there by the outboard, I wondered how much of the water in the bay had come from Mud Creek near our house, and I pictured the maps on which I'd traced the flow from Mud Creek as it coursed to Fall Creek, down to White River, over to the Wabash, down to the Ohio, on to the Mississippi, and finally to mix with the Gulf of Mexico which connected to this very bay. More than once, I'd dreamed of getting a canoe and following that waterway, fishing and camping as I went, paddling all the way to St. Pete to stay with my grandparents.

"The light! The light!" my father growled. "If you want to go out in this boat tomorrow, I need you to hold the goddamn light." He snatched it from me and aimed it. "There. Right there. See? Now hold it."

Despite my father, it was peaceful out there on the dock in the warm night air, water gently lapping at the seawall. At the far end of the bay, a high bridge arched across the horizon, the lights of cars crossing like illuminated insects on a branch. A few boats plied the bay with their red and green lights. Then I heard an odd slurping noise, not quite like a fish jumping. I glanced around but assumed it was the wake of a passing boat against the sea wall. Then again, slurp, slurp. I saw something in the water. I shined the flashlight out there and saw a pair of dolphins swimming around not twenty yards off the dock.

"Hey," my father snapped.

"Look! Look!" I said. And my father saw them too.

"Hey, Ellen!" he called to my mother, "Girls!" The whole family came out, my mother, my sisters and brother, my grandparents, and we all stood on the dock in silence but for a whisper about how wonderful or beautiful as the dolphins circled past a few more times, putting on a private show before disappearing into the night.

Though we watched for them every day and night after that, we never saw the dolphins again.

That night Chris and I slept in the boat with the sound of the water lapping the hull and the sea wall. I'd never spent a night aboard a boat in the water, in a bay connected to the open ocean, in a bay with real dolphins, and it took me a long time to fall asleep from the excitement of it. The next morning, I woke up and lay there listening to the water. When I got up, I gave out a yell. My feet splashed down into knee deep water!

Chirs, never a morning person, opened one eye, grumbled, "Shut–the–hell–up."

"We're sinking," I yelled.

That got Chris's attention. We scrambled up on the dock, dumping our buckets of crabs into the bay and started bailing. My grandmother came outside and said with a laugh, "What's all the commotion?" When she saw the water, she got my father.

My old man was pissed. "What the hell did you do?"

"Woke up to your sinking ship," my brother said.

"Watch your mouth." He kicked off his shoes and joined us. "Gimme that bucket." He grabbed it out of my hands and commenced bailing, slinging the water way out into the bay as if it were a contest. Or as if the further he threw it, the longer it would take to find its way back in. "Outta the way. Outta the way," he barked at me with a shove, and I climbed out of the boat and sat on the edge of the dock, awaiting orders.

My grandfather tottered out, pipe in hand, and watched for a few seconds, tapping the bowl of his pipe against the butt of his hand and blowing through the stem, then tapping a few more times. "Looks like she's sprung a leak, Dale."

My father ignored him.

"Did you check your plug, Son?"

"Of course I checked the plug, Dad," my father snapped. "You think I'm some goddamn kind of idiot?"

I looked up at my grandfather. He raised his eyebrows. "No, I just know sometimes the simplest thing ..." The pipe went back to his mouth and I heard air whistling through it as he blew on the stem again and surveyed the bay. He glanced down at me, "Going to be another beautiful day in the Sunshine State, Matthew." Then he watched my father and brother again, "Dale? What do you suppose the problem is?"

"I DON'T KNOW!"

My grandfather put his empty pipe in his mouth and strolled off the dock back inside. As soon as he did, I noticed my father checking the plug, and muttering, "Sure as hell ain't the goddamn plug."

My mother stepped out from the screen door. "Boys?" she called. "You come on in and have some breakfast. Let your father work on the boat."

Before getting out of the cabin cruiser, Chris skimmed up a bit of the milky saltwater and threw it on me.

Unable to get the engine started, my father got a neighbor to tow him over to the marina. While the rest of us went back to the beach, keeping t-shirts on, the old man spent the day putting a fiberglass patch on the hull. It had probably cracked from the jolt when the trailer lost a wheel. That night the boat was back. The engine was still balky, but someone at the marina had sold my father a bunch of parts sure to fix the problem.

So the next day, while the rest of us went to Sea World and let sunburn heal, my father replaced parts on the decrepit Johnson outboard. That night before dinner, he announced the boat was ready for a family outing. We all suppressed doubt and sent up a cheer.

It was dusk by the time we were ready to go. We males of the clan were excited for the adventure. My mother shared a glance with my grandparents that said, 'I hope this works out okay', but she was a good sport and climbed aboard. At the last moment, my grandparents demurred, staying on the end of the dock. My father ordered Chris to shove off before anyone could ask them a second time.

On the second try, the old Johnson rumbled to life. Another cheer, and we were motoring across the bay. Dad pushed the outboard to its limit, and though it ran rough, we cruised at a pretty good clip. He slowed down, circled around past my grandparents so we could all wave to each other, and we headed out toward the high-arching bridge, out toward the wide open Gulf of Mexico. Just before we reached the bridge and the promise of open sea, WHAM. We jolted to a stop. The family fell all over the boat. My sisters screamed with laughter. Mom got angry. And the engine slammed to a stop.

Some fishermen by the bridge were laughing. I noticed how my father glared at them and imagined he'd love to punch a nose. One of the fishermen called out: "You hit the sand bar, Buddy." My father jumped overboard and shoulder-to-the-bow hefted the boat off the sand bar, and climbed back in. He tried to start the engine. No go. He messed with it while we drifted, all of us in silence. Finally our father got the engine started. Another cheer–this one lacking energy. But when he started forward–clam, bam. He'd hit the sand bar again. Over the side he went, cussing a blue streak and pushed us off. He had more trouble getting the engine started, and when he finally did, it ran so rough it practically jumped off the mount. Now when the engine revved, the boat didn't move. He tilted the outboard up to check, and we'd sheered off two-thirds of the propeller.

And so we drifted on the tide until a good Samaritan towed us back. My grandparents came out on the dock as we tied up the boat, but my father stormed right past them, got in the Caddy, and sped off, leaving my mother to explain.

The next day Chris and I took the Fleetwood to Sarasota, him cursing the rolling icon of the Establishment (and probably the fact that he had to bring his kid brother along), to pick up his buddy and go see a spring training baseball game. It was the first major league game I ever saw. The Chicago White Sox beat the Cleveland Indians. Meanwhile, our father went out and got another propeller, determined to make good and prove that bringing the boat wasn't a wasted effort, even though we only had two days of vacation left.

Replacing the propeller was a problem too. He tried to replace it with the outboard tipped up out of the water and fumbled the prop into the bay. To retrieve it, my six-foot-one, 240-pound father, put on my kid-sized goggles–looking like a living cartoon with the small oval on his large head and bulky torso–and flopped over the side backward in Jacques Cousteau fashion. But he found the prop. Then he put on two ski belts and bobbed around the bay with my goggles on top of his head like a beanie as he refit the outboard with the new propeller.

Hot dog, we were ready for the open sea.

But the sand bar had broken something in the outboard and it never ran again.

*

At the end of spring break week the boat had to be towed back to the marina in defeat. The Cadillac was hooked up to it (like an albatross around my father's neck), and he towed it back to my grandparents' house. For our last night in Florida, like our first, Chris and I slept in the boat parked in the driveway.

Early the next morning we loaded up. Chris returned to a Dramamine–oblivion, and my sisters whispered and laughed softly. Me? I took my place, once more simmering in the heat flowing between my parents.

On the way home, we stopped early enough to stay at a Best Western. In that glamorous room, I realized what a dump The

Rainbow Motor Lodge had been. No one else was interested in the pool, so I went for a swim alone, and Mom sat on the edge of the pool to watch.

"What do you think, Matt?" She said. "Was the trip worth it? Going all that way?"

"Oh, yeah," I said, swimming up and holding the edge of the pool next to her. "The beach was great. The ballgame was great. Seeing the dolphins in the bay and at Sea World? All great." I then thought of the shells I'd collected and the little stuffed alligator I'd bought–which I already had mixed emotions about, thinking of them killing baby alligators for stupid Northern tourists. "Yeah, it was great," I said. "Think we can come back next year?"

Mom laughed and looked at the sky. "I don't know about that. We'll see." Then she added: "No boats and no Cadillac."

"Right," I said. "We still have tomorrow. Think we can go to Lookout Mountain?"

She pulled down her sunglasses and gave me a look.

"Thanks for the trip, Mom. I know it hasn't always been fun for you."

"That's kind of the way it goes. Especially when your father gets one of his crazy ideas," she said with a half grin.

"Or two crazy ideas."

*

Along the road I had eyed the billboards luring tourists to spectacular sites, but only two interested me: Mammoth Cave and Lookout Mountain (See Seven States!). My parents, and my siblings, relented on Lookout Mountain, Tennessee–Patty and Jo nixed any notion of crawling around in a cave.

Dad wanted to stay the course, to get home before dark, but Mom said we could all use a break, and we were going to Lookout Mountain. Dad started to object, but she cut him off–"A beautiful spot in your old home state, Dale," she said with the slightest nudge of her elbow against me. I returned the nudge and looked up at her. Without returning my glance, she gave a second nudge.

Up the winding mountain road the Fleetwood pulled the boat. The far-reaching view at the top of the stairs was cool, and I liked the map showing the states you could see from there, but what drew me in was the history of the Civil War battle to control the mountain top. They called it Battle Above the Clouds because the mountain was socked in with a thick fog the day of the Union attack. Although clear and sunny the day of our visit, I could feel the lack of clarity and confusion of that fog. The Union had finally taken the mountain in a bloody campaign. At the gift shop, I nearly bought a pennant showing the seven states, but set it aside when I saw a shoebox full of what looked like rocks at first glance; they were actual Civil War bullets. I picked up a thumb-sized hunk of lead partially mangled from whatever it had hit, a misshapen football of lead. The spent bullets were $1.00 each. I bought one.

From the gift shop, I went to the museum area, reading about the battle and studying the photographs. I fingered the bullet in my pocket as I went. What was the story of this bullet? Did it hit a man? Was it fired by a Union sniper picking off Rebs with an early repeater rifle? Or maybe it was fired in a blind flurry of fear by someone running for his life while his friends fell around him.

Then I wandered alone down onto the battlefield, finding some of the very stone outcroppings where victorious Union soldiers were photographed over a hundred years earlier–including the one where Abraham Lincoln had been photographed, standing a head taller than his soldiers. I stood on the very stone where Lincoln stood, trying to feel the greatness he had brought there. I'd read that some drummer boys were only 12 years old, same age as me. Standing out there, I imagined myself among the men fighting, firing at close range, and struggling in hand-to-hand combat with knives and swords and bayonets. I also imagined the unarmed drummer boys, pounding their drums as mini-balls whizzed around them.

It made me think about wars. I had heard about kids getting killed in war and about kids being soldiers somewhere in Africa and Asia. My father, who loved war movies and romanticized himself fighting in war, wished he'd been old enough for World War II. And while he railed against anti-military types, he never entered the military himself.

"There he is," I heard my father say. "Come on, Matt, let's go."

Then my mother came up beside him, "No, Dale," she said. Then she turned to me, "Look around a bit if you want, Matt. It's okay. We'll be up here by the shop. Take your time." Then she led my father away.

Somehow she sensed that her sixth-grade boy who rejected textbook learning, especially history, was learning here. She knew the power of a daydream. Many times I'd watched her pause to stare off into space, pondering something, dreaming of something.

I climbed an outcropping and sat to look across the battlefield. I thought about the Civil War. And about Viet Nam. How were they similar? Then I thought of my parents, my family; how was it like the conflicts I sensed there?

Who was right? Who would win?

Then I saw the Fleetwood pulling the cabin cruiser down the road by the battlefield. A fear that I thought I'd outgrown flared now as I saw them driving away. Since I was a little kid, I was sure my family would forget about me and leave me behind since Patty and Jo and Chris were so much more valuable, so much more important. I was sure it would happen, maybe on purpose since I was in the way, another expense without adding any value, without doing anything new to be proud of, like Patty and Jo being the first in the family to go to college, and Chris being the first to make All County in two sports. My siblings still teased me for being the one who had caused those intercom announcements in discount stores: "Would the mother of a little boy named Matty, with the blue-and-white striped T-shirt and curly brown hair, please come to Customer Service...." My irritated mother or mortified sisters would come to get me. Here on Lookout Mountain at age 12, that old fear fluttered at the sight of the rolling Fleetwood.

I ran across the battlefield, chasing the big car pulling the cabin cruiser. As I ran I imagined myself a drummer boy racing for cover. My chest hurt, and I sprinted and sprinted, racing for my place to sit between my parents. Despite the heat of my mother's quiet anger toward my father for cutting short my reverie, and despite his hostility and anger at waiting for a stupid kid to finish wandering around with his head in the past, I needed to sit between them. Was that my job, my role, my value to the family–to hold together this imperfect union?

The Dog Lover

I'd always wanted a dog. But my mother had allergies when I was a boy, and then my wife didn't like them. So at thirty-eight, I was as excited as a kid when a forklift approached carrying a plastic crate. Above the wire door, it said "Zappy," and I saw the nickel-colored Weimaraner inside. This was going to be fun, baby-sitting my best friend's dog. I knew Megan would love the pointer too. After the initial surprise. She'd never been around a real dog—nothing but those fluffy-white yappers her mother kept. No wonder she wasn't a dog lover.

Waiting at the American Air Cargo Center in East Boston on that freezing cold January night, I believed, or hoped, that Kevin's dog had swooped down out of the night sky to become the glue that would hold my wife and me together in that rocky year. It was worth a shot after eight years of marriage. Kevin, a guy I've known since nap-time, had planned to take the dog along when he directed a documentary movie about Chaucer's England but learned that the British quarantine dogs for six months. The dog nut couldn't leave his little boo-boo in a kennel with a 20-foot fenced run, so he asked me to take care of her for the five months he'd be gone.

When I asked Megan about dog sitting, she said, "No way, Bob. Absolutely not."

Now, Megan is the sort of woman who frequently says yes when she means no, and no when she means yes. Though this was not such a case. Still, I believed her 'no' would melt into a 'yes' after a day or two of tail-wagging, unconditional love. In time, she'd thank me.

Another notion played in the back of my mind. If Megan and I separated before June, I wouldn't have to move out since most apartments don't take dogs. Not that I wanted her to leave, but if things went sideways, who doesn't want a contingency plan?

The woman working the cargo counter suggested I take the dog out while she processed the paperwork. I looked through the one-inch wire squares of the crate door, and pale green eyes locked on me, like something out of a horror movie. Kevin had renamed his dog Zappy (from Spot) after the puppy chewed through an electrical cord and got shocked. I wondered if the jolt had given her those green eyes. Before we went out, I checked the weather app on my iPhone–ten degrees in Boston that night with six inches of fresh snow on the parking lot and a frigid wind whipping off the harbor. I pulled my collar up and pulled Zappy into the cold. This Los Angeles dog, never exposed to temperatures below 50 degrees, stepped through the snow as if it were knee-deep molasses. Zappy did her business, and as we headed back toward the office, a guy came out and yelled, "I hope you don't plan to leave that there."

I had nothing with which to scoop the poop. Beginning to question my commitment to dog-sitting, I packed snow around Zappy's steaming relief and rushed for the dumpster.

As I signed papers, Kevin's dog shivered at my feet like one of those electric football games I had as a kid, practically vibrating around the room.

I led her out to the car and opened the back door. "Okay, Zappy ju–" and she sprang effortlessly into the back seat. "Good girl," I said shutting the door. I wrestled the crate into the trunk which I had to tie part-way open. Before I could get in, the silver beast scrambled into the driver's seat. I shoved her across the console into the passenger seat, taut muscles quivering under my fingers, and I got in. Like a bumble bee on speed, Zappy's nose bounced–bing, bing, bing–my hair, neck, ears, hands, crotch, and the car's dashboard, steering wheel, gear shift–taking an olfactory inventory of everything.

What had I gotten myself into? I already wanted to mark the calendar for Kevin's return and my ETL (Estimated Time of Liberation): June, five months away. The trees would be green, t-shirts replacing parkas. Driving through blowing snow to the North Shore, spring seemed as distant as Oz. But on the other hand, a showdown with Megan, seemed all too close.

I went in the back door, holding the dog's collar. I could hear the TV, Megan watching Jimmy Fallon as she did most nights–not because she liked him, I knew, but because her boss did and often referred to Fallon's jokes the next day. When Megan answered my "hello," Zappy exploded from my grasp and raced in to see her. My wife screamed at the sight of this metal-colored monster, fighting off the dog as it sniffed her head to toe. And then it was off, bounding all over the house–the bee on speed in a larger garden–sniffing every corner, every piece of furniture, every everything. Megan shrieked at me while I pursued the beast. The more Megan understood, the angrier she got, and I soon realized she was chasing me while I was chasing the dog. We all stopped in the kitchen when the dog assumed the position and let go on the kitchen floor.

That's when Megan punched me in the back of the head. Later she swore she didn't, insisting it was only a push ("a little Bobby bump" I think she called it), but it sure felt like a punch.

The dog vanished while I cleaned up the poop. Megan stood over me demanding answers. How on earth could I take the dog after she'd said no? The last thing our marriage needed was to throw a dog into the mix. What kind of person did that?

"Kevin was desperate," I lied. "How could I deny my oldest friend? He's always been there for me."

Megan stomped upstairs. I half expected her to pack her bags. Then I heard her yelling and ran upstairs to find Megan, hands on her hips at the bathroom door, Zappy cowering in the bath tub. "The toothpaste, Bob! I saw this monster eat the toothpaste, tube and all!"

"You'll just have to use a little soap."

"Great! Perfect!" Megan screamed. "Except that insane dog ate the soap too!"

Then I noticed the bathroom trash was also empty, not even a thread of dental floss left. I practically gagged. "Let me get her crate. Kevin told me to have her sleep in her crate." I ran for the car.

When I came back in with the big plastic box, Megan said, "Not in my kitchen."

Ever since we used her Fidelity bonus two years ago to remodel it, the kitchen was *hers*. We eighth-grade history teachers don't get bonuses, not that Megan understood that. Last fall she suggested I go in and ask for a raise, and she had a hard time believing there wasn't a way around scheduled pay increases for teachers. Life was different for middle-managers at Fidelity Investments. The year she started making more money than I did, our relationship got a little wonky. Her clothes got nicer, for example, and I sensed a growing distain for my post–grunge, neo–hipster style of battered jeans and flannel shirts. I believe she once referred to it as my slacker uniform. She insisted her higher income and ambitions had nothing to do with her new "investments" in work fashion.

A lot had changed since we first met, and clothes were the least of it. Back then we were both in our mid–twenties, both part–time grad students at UMass Boston, who met over brown–bag dinners in the library cafeteria. Megan was getting her MBA, me teaching and getting my masters in education. Life was simple. Life was fun.

Anyway, I started upstairs, bumping the big plastic crate against the walls, when I heard Megan yell, "Not in our bedroom, Bob." That left the guest room or the den, so I waited a few back–aching seconds. "Put it in the guest room," she hollered. Fine, how fitting for our long term guest.

I opened the bathroom door to discover that the monster had chewed a hole in the shampoo bottle and was lapping up the shampoo like gravy. Welcome, Zappy!

Why had I agreed to this? By the time I got the dog in her crate and sat down in the den to read Kevin's instructions: "The Tao of Zappy," it was after midnight. Then the phone rang, Kevin calling to check on his dog.

"Tell me," I said, "does she often crap on the floor?"

"Oh, no, she must be stressed from the flight. She never does that. I'm sorry, Bob."

"Let's talk about stress," I said. I knew he'd feel bad, which pinched me with guilt. Yet I couldn't help but add, "Kev, does her diet often include toothpaste, a bar of soap, bathroom trash and shampoo?"

"Didn't you read my letter?" No apology this time.

"Just getting to it when you called. It's been a little wild around here," I said. "I thought this would be fun."

"It will be. She's screwed up from the flight. Zappy's a great dog, Bob. You'll see."

Reading Kevin's detailed instructions for the dog's care, I realized this dog was more trouble than a kid.

Kids. Long ago, Megan and I had agreed not to have any. Although, once in a while, I did think having a baby would be nice, a child who loved me, us, someone to nurture and guide from her first steps through college graduation (whenever I daydreamed of having a child, it was always a little girl). When I brought it up a few times, Megan scotched the discussion in seconds.

I turned the page in "The Tao of Zappy" and discovered the last, and longest, section of the letter, titled: "My Failures in Training."

I didn't like the sound of it.

Kevin opened with a warning that Weimaraners in general, and Zappy in particular, are difficult because of "a propensity to perpetually test the rules." For example, over the last few years, Zap had leaped up on the kitchen counter and consumed: an entire chocolate cake, lasagna, bananas, nuts, a bag of flour (yes, a whole bag of flour), as well as used aluminum foil and cellophane. Kevin wasn't sure what else she'd eat because he no longer left anything out. He also listed the bathroom items with which I'd had first hand experience.

*

Megan and I, and our marriage, survived the first two weeks. But Megan's anger gleamed anew when Zappy committed any offense, like the day Zap chewed the fingers off one of Megan's red leather gloves. The constant vigilance over the dog exhausted us, but it also united us–the way a grizzly at the door would refocus a quarreling pioneer couple.

I found things to appreciate about Zappy. In the evenings she curled up at my feet, sometimes on my feet. When we had a fire in our wood-burning stove, she slept next to it, feet twitching with dreams of running in the woods. At playtime, she raced after her rope toy, sliding around corners, leaping over furniture. Toss a tennis ball outside and she made soaring, acrobatic catches. Lob a snowball and she'd catch it shattering in her mouth, gobbling up whatever was left and racing back for more.

Since it was a snowy winter, I bought a pair of cross-country skis, something I'd wanted to try for years, and I loved it. With stride-and-glide in the great outdoors (Zap racing out ahead and back and out ahead again), I forgot any stresses about teaching history to 126 gum-snapping eighth graders. And those about Megan. When not skiing, I took Zap for long walks in the woods and on the golf course. As a side benefit, I got in better shape. Even bought a Fitbit and synced it to my iPhone to track it.

At the snow-covered golf course, I stood around with other dog walkers discussing doggie psychology while the canines romped in the snow. I took pride—a bizarre pride, I admit—when other owners marveled at Zappy's athleticism and boundless energy. She was my Michael Jordan to their Dagwood Bumsteads.

As life got better with the dog, I also saw it getting better between Megan and me. We fought less. Squabbling over petty matters, like how to hang bathroom towels, all but ended. My hope that Zap might unite us was coming true. Even our communication, never a strength, improved a tad—hell, more than a tad. Funny how that happened when we stopped eating dinner in front of the TV where Lester Holt did all the talking. In the living room, Zap begged. In the dining room, she didn't (one of Kevin's successes in training). So we ate at the dining room table and talked.

"How was your day?" I asked again.

"Fine." Then she leaned in, a forkful of rice pilaf suspended between us, and said: "What do you *need* in a relationship, Bob?"

I took a bite of chicken thigh. "Did you make the chicken differently tonight?"

"Shake-N' Bake, the new Herbs and Spice style," she said. I nodded, gnashing off another hunk of chicken as she continued: "Bob, I was wondering, what your long-term goals are? Personally and professionally?"

Chewing, I held the chicken up, "I knew it was different. I like the extra zing."

Pursing up her mouth, she closed her eyes and shook her head.

"Okay, okay," I said. "My professional goal is to teach history. That's what I do. I've achieved my goal. I like it a lot. And I plan to keep doing it."

"But you complain about it a lot," she said. "Don't you want to move up? Make more money, or try something new?"

"Everybody complains about work, right? You should hear talk in the Teachers' Lounge," I said. "And every year I try new things. This year we created a class play about Lee's surrender to Grant at Appomattox. Then my kids in History Club are doing real research at the Historical Society to write a paper about the role of slavery in post–Revolutionary New England. As for moving up, there's nowhere to go but administration. And I have zero interest in that." Dissatisfaction registered all over her face.

"What about you, then, Megan?" I asked.

"Professionally, I have three goals...." And she rattled them off and how to achieve each as if she'd just come from a Fidelity goals-management seminar. Perhaps she had. What they amounted to was make more money, get more power in the company, and kick Vanguard's butt.

"Personally," she said and paused before going on, "I have goals too."

"I'm sure you do," I responded, hoping for some interruption, a phone call, an insurance salesman at the door, a Zap attack–anything.

"I don't really want to get into them, Bob," she paltered, so I knew she was dying to share. When I didn't respond, she began. She wanted a larger house in a more prestigious suburb (which meant I couldn't ride my bike to work); she wanted a nicer car for me (never mind that my twelve–year–old Honda suited me fine);

she wanted our personal and professional ambitions to mesh better; and she wanted to rekindle both the passion and the friendship in our marriage.

I was at once relieved and disappointed that she didn't mention wanting a baby. Even if I'd known what my personal goals were, I never got to mention them.

But as we cleared the table, I did manage to slip in this gem:

"One person's complacency is another's contentment," I said, kind of proud of myself.

"Yeah," she answered, "I've heard that one before."

I was pretty sure I'd made it up on the fly but didn't quibble.

*

When it came time to ship Zappy back to L.A., Megan and I took her to the airport. Our last walk was around the same parking lot that had had six inches of snow on it when I picked up Zap on that frigid January night. In the first week of June, it was warm and sunny. When I locked Zappy in the crate–poking my fingers through the wire door to let her lick them–I felt the heartache of a parent putting his child on a bus for summer camp in Maine. But Zap was never coming back.

On the way home, Megan began to cry. I patted my wife on the thigh and said, "She'll be all right."

"I'm not worried about *her*, Bob," Megan said and turned to face the window.

The next week, the house felt vacant while Megan and I passed each other in a kind of shared solitude. I quit wearing my Fitbit since I wasn't walking Zappy any more, and it was deflating to see digital reminders that pegged me as a couch potato. Once again Megan and I ate dinners on TV-trays and let Lester Holt do the talking. It was clear that we had lost more than a dog when we shipped Zappy back. What it was exactly, I could not say. But apparently Megan had a pretty good idea because when I returned from my last day of school before summer, she sat in her kitchen waiting. Before I could say 'you're home early', she said she was leaving.

"But we were getting along so well," I said. "We'd fallen back in love."

"You fell in love with a dog, Bob."

"No, no, no. What about our new-found interests."

"Interests? We share no interests. We just cohabitate."

"*Peacefully*," I clowned, with a finger in the air, as if making her smile would make her stay.

"Yes, peacefully," she acknowledged, "and passionlessly."

"It was not the dog I fell in love with. It was that the dog helped me, helped us, rediscover each other. I've been thinking. If we had a baby, it would do the same thing. Be our unifying force."

"Forget it, Bob. I told you, no kids. Especially not now. It's over."

She started out of the room, but I stepped in front of her. "I'm not letting you go."

She glared at me, a danger in her look. "I want to keep this clean and polite, so don't push me. There's nothing here to keep me." And she shouldered past as if I were a swinging door.

"You'll be back in two days," I said.

"Don't bet on it."

"Megan, you still love me, and I still love you."

She turned, "I don't respect you any more, Bob," she said, "and I can't even like, let alone love, a man I don't respect. If you were honest, you'd admit that you loved that dog more than me."

I slumped into a chair at the kitchen table, stinging from the candor of her saying she had no respect for me. This was hard to hear because, as a teacher, I wanted more than anything for my students to respect me, and here my own wife didn't. Equally painful was her proclamation that I had deluded myself about my love for her.

Megan returned to the dining room with a duffel bag slung over her shoulder and a large hanging bag in her hands. She went out to the garage and, following her, I saw her Volvo stuffed to the windows. Yes, she was going. "That's the last of it for now," she said. "I'll arrange to come with a U-Haul for the rest."

Feeling my posture go slack, my tie swinging away from my chest, I zombied back inside behind her. In the kitchen, Megan began a prepared, cliché-riddled speech about this being the best thing for both of us, no one to blame, different life goals, fresh starts, and so on. "There's one more thing before I go," she said.

I held out a fillet knife for her.

"Stop that." She took the knife and put it on the counter.

"Come on, Bob," she said, "there's somebody I want you to meet." I followed her onto the deck where she surveyed the backyard. "Sam?" she called. I expected her new boyfriend to step out and shake my hand, Mr. Magnanimous of Greater Boston. Instead, a silver Weimaraner puppy trotted out of the flowers with an up-rooted iris in its mouth. "Honey," she said, "meet Sam."

"You're leaving me for Sam?"

"No, I'm leaving you *with* Sam, Samantha. She's yours. Kevin helped me get her from the same California breeder and the same mother as Zappy. She was too much for the woman who owned her. But after Zappy, I figured she'd be a snap for you."

I went into the yard to see the gangly puppy. The cute little imp jumped away and then played tug-of-war with the iris. After a little romping, I hoisted her, and she playfully chewed my thumb. "Oh, you're a big baby aren't you?" I said and began to thank Megan but turned just in time to see her tail lights at the end of the driveway. As Megan rolled into the street, I felt the other edge of her gesture, and it cut me deeply, making me want to cry out that I did love her, and I really could make her happy. But right then Samantha gave me a big slobbery lick on the ear, and I had to laugh.

Enter Debbie DeVore

"Hey, you!" a girl's voice yelled.

I was on my bike, riding fast for the lake to go fishing. It was close to 9:00, getting a late start. But I hit the brakes when I heard her voice and circled back. I knew who it was, Debbie DeVore. She was sixteen. I was fourteen, just finished eighth grade. Debbie wore a tight, orange t-shirt–no bra. It ended at the waistband of her cutoff blue jeans, cut short to show off her long, thin legs.

"Where are you going in such a hurry?" she asked.

She had these intense blue eyes, and her dark brown hair hung straight down in a hippie style. I had trouble keeping my eyes off her nipples which rose up in the cool morning air, pointing right at me.

"Well?" she repeated, hands to her hips. "Where you heading?"

"Up to the reservoir to go fishing. Then maybe a swim." I imagined her swimming in those short shorts and that little t-shirt—no bra.

"Ever go skinny dipping?" she asked.

I couldn't believe she asked, asked like it was nothing. I'd never heard a girl ask a question like that, and I couldn't answer. I did go skinny dipping, most fishing days. Mom didn't want me to swim alone, but I did, skinny dipping because I couldn't wear wet shorts home. There were no houses around the lake, just woods. A couple of times fishermen saw me skinny dipping and hooted, but I didn't care. A girl though... Debbie DeVore, skinny dipping? Only in my dreams.

"Jason? You okay?"

Jason? Debbie DeVore knew my name?

I guess it made sense, we'd ridden the school bus together for a year. We rode together in the morning, first ones on, last ones off, because we lived out in the country. We junior high kids rode to the high school to drop off Debbie and the other high schoolers, then rode to our school. On the way home, we got on first and then picked up the high school kids. My ride was close to an hour each way. Debbie and I had talked a little on the bus, but not much, mostly me calling out a fox I might see at the edge of a field or a deer, or saying goodbye at the end of the day. She never spoke to me in the morning.

"Sorry, yeah, I'm still half asleep," I answered.

"Tell me about it," she said.

She did look like she'd just gotten up. But I was lying. I'd been up for over two hours, to, as Mom said, "finish chores before fishing."

"How do you like it out here?" I asked, changing the subject. What a stupid question, I thought. The DeVores had moved from the suburbs out here to the country the previous summer. I was sure Debbie hated it.

"It's all right," she said. "If I don't die of boredom." Then she leaned in close, with this sexy look in her eye: "But in July, I get my license, so I'll be free."

She crossed her arms, and I realized I was looking at her nipples again. Hard not to–because I was a horny fourteen–year–old, but also, they pointed at me like two fingers. "Double–D," guys called her. She was not busty, but they called Debbie DeVore that anyway, because, well, because we were junior high idiots. Horny little idiots. Some of the crude dudes from Oaklandon even called her "DeVore the whore."

People called Oaklandon kids "hillbillies," but I never did. When my mom was a kid and her family moved up from southeastern Kentucky, people called them hillbillies, and she hated that term, so you never heard it in our house. My mother shook off the Kentucky accent, but when she was tired or ticked off, you'd hear it come back.

Anyhow, Debbie DeVore was no whore, and no DD bra size, but something sexy emanated from her. She knew it, and she used it.

Within a week, Debbie and I were an item. I couldn't believe my luck. But I kind of could. Like me, she was bored, curious, and horny. Her parents both worked. Her older brother worked. Her other boyfriend–who was seventeen–worked. She hung around reading magazines and watching lousy daytime TV.

I was a suitable distraction.

Unless I had to work at one of the local farms or pick parts for my old man, I got up early to go fishing. Afterwards, I'd sneak in through the DeVore's back door using the key Debbie had given me, and head up to her bedroom to wake her up. And we went skinny dipping at the lake a couple of times.

I learned a lot that summer.

I stole a copy of *Everything You Wanted to Know about Sex but Were Afraid to Ask*, and Debbie and I took turns reading it out loud to each other. We laughed and cringed and experimented. Then I stole a copy of *The Happy Hooker*, and that made Debbie crazy mad. Was it the "DeVore the whore" connection? She snatched it out of my hand and threw it at me. I ducked. Then she grabbed it and rammed it in the garbage. Okay, message received.

That was also the summer I gave up baseball–which pissed off my older brother–because I wanted to spend more time fishing. I also worked part time at two farms, Korn's Christmas Tree Farm and the Parker farm. Occasionally, I also worked at a small orchard near home–although I was paid in apples. Ever since I was five, Mom had snapped a paper bag to signal me to walk the half mile to the orchard where I could pick apples off the ground. We'd have apples every night from the early, gnarly green ones to the final red ones that hung on until they turned mealy under December snows.

But my main preoccupation that summer was Debbie DeVore.

When she got her license, we began to venture farther and farther from home. She'd drop her mother off at work, swing by and pick me up down the road from home, and we were gone. We drove to Butler where we walked around campus and pretended to be college kids (I'm sure I fooled no one). Then on to IU where my older brother went, and up to Purdue where Debbie's parents had met. One day in early August, she picked me up at a meeting spot down Mud Creek Road.

"Where to today?" I asked.

She kissed me. "Cincinnati, Ohio!"

"What?" It hadn't dawned on me we could cross the state line. My mom would kill me. But only if she found out.

"Let's go," I said. And we had an adventure, exploring the city, walking the serpentine wall along the Ohio River and watching barges pass. We went uptown to the University of Cincinnati and had a late lunch of Skyline Chili.

Coming home, we knew we'd cut it close. We stopped for gas and a pop in Batesville, Indiana–"Casket Making Capitol of America." Debbie still had to pick up her mother at work. When we came out, the back tire was flat. Debbie immediately started crying. "My mom will kill me. I'm dead."

"At least we're in the Casket Capitol of America," I said, but she saw no humor in it.

"Why are you crying?"

"We don't know how to change a tire!"

"I do," I said, and got busy.

I thought I was her big hero, but when I leaned across the seat, hand on her thigh–

"Don't," she said. "Your hands are filthy."

She was right, but I thought dirty heroes were sexy to girls. "Let me run in and wash up," I said, but she was already rolling.

The car was quiet with the air conditioner humming, but we didn't talk much as she drove fast. The radio played. I could see she was worried about meeting her mom late.

But it felt like something more.

When we got close to Indianapolis, Debbie said, "Where can I drop you off?"

"What?"

"I can't take you home," she said, "I'm already late to pick up my mom."

"Right, but I can't ride with you?"

"No," she said. "She doesn't know I see you."

That put me off. Not about her mom, but I got the sense I wasn't good enough for Debbie DeVore. Like her family would think poorly of me. Would they? Did they?

I didn't say anything, and she kept driving. We were close to downtown. "Can I let you off here?"

"I don't even know where we are," I said.

"You're smart. You'll figure it out," she said.

"What?"

"Just get out, Jason! I'm late to get my mom, you idiot!"

So I got out, and she sped away from the curb. That was how it ended.

I saw Debbie a few days later. I stopped by to return her house key, and we went out on the back deck. She was cool to me. I was cool to her.

"Guess it's over?" I finally said.

"I think so," she answered. She came up close and leaned in with those killer blue eyes looking up at me. "But it was fun while it lasted, right?" Her hand went to the front of my jeans and rubbed lightly. "Mmmm," she said to the rise in my pants. I was confused and thought we were back on or ready for some fun. "I have one favor to ask," she whispered. "Let's keep this summer fling between us. It will be better for your freshman year if people don't know."

Better for me? Or better for you? I wanted to ask, but I didn't have the guts.

We had one long, long, deep kiss–like she'd taught me. As I tried to go to the next step, she gently held me off. "No, Jason." She smiled. "I have to go now." And she stepped away.

When school started, Debbie DeVore was a junior. I was a freshman. She drove to school. I took the bus. In busy halls at school, she never seemed to recognize me. But she knew me, and I knew her.

The Chain Saw Artist

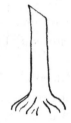

"For crying out loud, Beth, we're not talking about college," Mason said. "We're talking about a chain saw."

"Fine," she said and walked on.

Mason followed, remembering her hair before she cut it, how she used to wear it in a chestnut-colored ponytail, and how the swing of it had always aroused him. He jogged to catch her, but once again she cantered half a step ahead. The pace had to hurt with her feet pinched into those pumps.

With each opening at The Bouche Gallery over the last year—and this had been the fourth: "Three Hoosier Postmodernists"—Beth had shed some awkwardness as she'd acquired new poses, gestures, and tilts of the head, just as she'd adopted the hairstyle and wardrobe. But inside, *inside*, he believed she was still his Beth, not the "Elizabeth" employed at The Bouche Gallery.

At the same time, he had to admit it wasn't just the trappings of the art world Beth had adopted. She'd gotten good about the art and describing it to customers. More than once, he'd heard Beth admire an artist's use of color and composition. Or she'd explain how this artist was inspired by another famous one, but this artist had discovered her own path, with color and shape that were all her own. Beth knew where the artists were from, where they'd studied, where their work had been shown, and if they were in museum collections or not.

He was impressed—and a little proud.

But on this night after the show, a big black dog of tension tagged along as she led them down Elm Street, Mason tried to enjoy the cool silence of the streets after midnight. Tomorrow would be an October Saturday, which meant sidewalks thick with fall-foliage tourists drifting in and out of Nema's shops—a living obstacle course while he delivered the mail from a bag heavy with Christmas catalogs.

"Wouldn't you love to own one of these big houses?" Beth said.

"Nah," Mason answered, recalling the heft of bills he delivered to the grand old brick and limestone homes. "I'd rather have a cabin in the woods on the far side of Hawks Lake."

"Not me," Beth said. After a moment she added, "I really do think you should finish college, Mason."

"An accounting degree won't buy you one of these houses."

"That's not why I want you to go back." She turned the next corner, heading for their street with its bungalows of vinyl and aluminum siding. "And it doesn't have to be accounting."

"I like my job, and I'm not going back to college. I'm happy with my house, and my town, and my girlfriend." Though, he'd been happier when she worked at the dress shop. He dared not ask if she was happy with him.

"We're not talking about our relationship," she said.

"What *are* we talking about?"

She didn't answer, and they were quiet until they got home. When Mason stood in front of her at the door and touched her shoulder, her muscles tensed under his hand. He tried to lift her jaw to look at her face, but she reared back. "I just wanted to talk about buying a stupid chain saw, and –" he said, hands gesturing that it had blown up in his face. "What happened?"

Beth sighed, "We need to sit down and have a long talk about it. But not tonight. I'm exhausted." She took the keys from his hand and unlocked the door. He followed her inside, and before she even unbuttoned her coat, she kicked off those pumps.

Talk about *it*, Mason thought. What *it*? Gene Bouche? Was she about to confess an affair? When she first worked at the gallery, she had always greeted Mason with a quick kiss when he delivered the mail. But now she vanished into the back room or slipped off to assist Gene or a customer as if ashamed of him. Occasionally, he was left with the odd impression that if he'd entered the gallery a moment sooner he'd have caught Beth and Gene touching. Mason noticed how she lingered near him. No doubt other people had too, and they were probably saying that Beth was sleeping with Gene Bouche, or if she wasn't, she soon would be. When Mason entered certain shops on Main Street lately, hadn't people stopped talking mid-sentence?

At the end of tonight's opening, Mason was helping Beth gather the oil-spotted napkins and plastic champagne glasses when Gene called, "Elizabeth," a rolling hand gesture reeling her over to talk with the artists. Mason went numb–the gesture was all Beth–he'd seen it a thousand times. And as she approached, Gene put his hand on her back with the ease of familiarity.

"What's going on, Beth?" he asked sitting in his favorite chair.

"We're different. That's all."

"After four years of living together, suddenly we're different?"

Mason asked.

"Not suddenly," she said. "Over the last few years, I've grown and changed, but you haven't."

"Since last year anyway."

"Don't blame the gallery or Gene. This was coming long before."

Maybe that was true. She was restless in a way, moving from the florist, to Eve's Dress Shop, now the gallery.

"Why do things have to change?" he asked. "What's wrong with settling into life and enjoying it?"

"Stagnating is not enjoyable for me, Mason."

"Stagnating? Now it's stagna–?"

"Think about it. You like your job, but that's all you've got. You have no interests or hobbies. Okay, you still play softball and watch sports on TV but that's no hobby. As a mailman, you don't create anything. The service never changes. The route never changes." She threw her coat on the sofa. "You're stuck in a rut, and you don't even see it. There's no forward movement to your life. That's why I nag you to go back to college. Not to get a bigger house, it's to get you to learn and grow."

She was on a roll. This little speech was rehearsed.

"Just because I'm not into every new fad–" He almost pointed out her recently cropped hair, new clothes, and asymmetrical jewelry but waved it off. "Look, we still get along, right?"

"What's to argue about? Do you care about anything enough to fight about it?" She waited. "Well?" hands to her hips. "Are you passionate about anything? Is there anything you'd die for?"

He wasn't going to answer this. He cared about things. But they were hard to put into words.

"Not arguing is no measure of a successful relationship," she added. And he wondered if she'd read that in one of her new magazines. "I love the gallery because the people there are changing, and growing, and creating. They're passionate." She sighed and sucked in a breath, then looked at him and held it.

"What?" he said. "Go ahead, say it all."

She nodded, tears welling up in her eyes. So now she was going to confess to having an affair and say she wanted to move out.

"You're boring, Mason." And she began to cry.

"That's it?"

"That's everything!"

She rushed from the living room and slammed the bathroom door. Mason flipped through her *Harpers*, waiting on the couch for her return. Would she say she'd outgrown him? But when he heard the shower start, he realized she'd already said so. Did she want to split up? After four great years together? What if they had married? Would vows and rings bind them together now?

It was not clear what he needed to do to keep her, but it was clear he needed to do something.

College? God, he'd hated it when he quit a hundred years ago. Besides, it would take time, and time was against him. Mason liked being Nema, Indiana's in-town mailman. Not many towns of 2,400 residents included wealthy retirees and Appalachianesque farmers, hippie holdouts and college professors, artists, laborers, antique dealers, and shopkeepers—all living in one valley. Making the rounds, exchanging talk of the weather with townspeople or scooping some gossip, those things fixed him in the clockworks of his community, an everyday cog maybe, but a real one. He shouldered the secrets of Nema, delivering cards, bills, and love letters. Even sub-zero January mornings provided an odd pleasure, wrapped in a parka and trudging in Sorells. Those frozen days ended with his feet warming by the woodstove. Oppressively hot muggy days in August often closed with a cooling dive into Hawks Lake—usually together with Beth. And the wondrous days of spring or fall, when the temperature settled in at 70 degrees behind a nice breeze, those days rewarded him beyond any brutal weather. Accepting a cup of hot tea with Mrs. Gardner on cold days, shooting a few baskets with two boys in a driveway, helping

Thelma hang Christmas lights around her shop window, pushing a car out of a snowbank, carrying a dozen pieces of Bazooka Bubble Gum to hand out to the kids he passed on the route–all of that had felt like enough.

It was enough. At least, he'd always thought so. Damn–it, he had a good job no matter what Beth thought or how much she wanted a sophisticated, college–educated boyfriend. She was the daughter of a roofer, living with a mailman–not so bad. The mortgage was in his name, so he covered property taxes and insurance, and as long as he covered his share of the bills, he shouldn't have to justify his job to her. And his share was the larger. Because he weighed 175 and she weighed 120, she made the wacky claim that he should pay more than half of the bills. Since he made more money, he didn't argue. Though he never saw how size had anything to do with the cost of mortgage, electricity, or heat.

College, Christ, he knew how to enjoy where he was in life. He knew the grass wasn't always greener on the other side of the fence. Stagnation my ass. What about satisfaction?

When Beth worked at Eve's Dress Shop, she never mentioned him changing jobs or going back to college. Then he had to go and tell her about the Bouche Gallery and suggest she apply for a job. She'd always loved art museums–could study a painting for a full minute or more. Mason liked art museums too, but he passed through galleries the way people flipped through a favorite magazine when he delivered it.

Every December, Mason and Beth went to Chicago for Christmas shopping and to visit The Art Institute. They both loved visiting Chicago, especially at Christmas time with the activity, lights, and sounds. Spontaneously they'd stop to hug and kiss on the street in parkas against the cold winds off the lake. Each day, they separated for a couple of hours to shop for each other. It was on their second–year trip to Chicago that Mason bought her an engagement ring.

He'd planned to give it to her on Christmas morning, but he was too excited to wait. When they stood before the large windows of the Blackstone Hotel, leaning against each other, watching snowflakes blow in over Lake Michigan, he pulled the box from his pocket and asked her to marry him.

She didn't take the box but gave him a huge hug and kissed his neck. "Oh, Mason," was all she said and held on to him. He laughed, thinking it was yes. She kissed him hard on the lips.

"Mason, this is so sweet, so wonderful," she said. "But no."

"No? Why not?"

"Because, because, because," she'd counted off on her fingers. Then she'd kissed him again and said she loved him and didn't want to screw it up. How about living together? She never did explain the three reasons, but Mason surmised that they tallied: her parents' lousy marriage, her sister's nasty divorce, and her best friend's abusive husband.

But none of that joy-of-the-job, take-pleasure-in-the-present, I'll-marry-you-someday crap mattered now. Something had to be done. To show her. To keep her. Time to smash the glass, kick the loyal dog, cross the line, leap the fence, head for the tall and uncut.

*

The next morning, Mason woke before the alarm sounded, and Beth wasn't there. He found her asleep on the sofa, curled like a cat under her coat. It was the first time in four years they hadn't slept in the same bed. Without waking her, he left for the post office.

After a long day on Saturday—navigating the hordes of fall foliage tourists which had lived up to his fear—he passed the window of Clifford's Hardware and looked in at the McCulloch chain saw he'd told Beth about. For the first time, he took note of the display. There stood a wooden bear about three feet tall, carved with a chain saw. Folk art. With one of those saws, Mason thought he could carve a bear like that. The cowbell clanged above Clifford's door and the floorboards, worn down to where the nail heads shone like chrome, creaked under Mason's feet. Ten minutes later, he scrawled a check, and headed for his cousin's farm in Sycamore Hollow. His half-ton Ford pickup bumped down the leaf-covered lane, tracing the edge of the meadow. When he saw the naked branches of a dead oak among the colorful leaves, he parked and entered the woods.

On the second pull, the McCulloch growled to life. Eyes squinted, lips drawn tight, Mason pressed the yellow-and-black McCulloch into the dead wood at shoulder height because he figured carving would be easier on a tree trunk. Sawdust showered over him, sticking to his skin, speckling his hair, and trickling down his chest at the opening of his blue-gray postman's shirt. And then the old oak made a slow quarter turn as it crashed into the undergrowth.

Ready to take on his first chain saw sculpture, Mason circled the stump—visualizing a bear like the one in the window of Clifford's Hardware. Then he started. Mindful that a moment's recklessness could ruin the carving, he rounded the head, a couple of bumps for ears. Extended forepaws like the display bear would be too difficult, so he cut the paws into the sides of the trunk. A lightweight saw maybe, but it got heavy with all the raising and lowering, twisting and turning. He roughed out the shoulders (one higher than the other, a small mistake), carved out the back (forgetting a tail) and then rounded the belly. With his shoulders aching and sweat dripping from his nose and eyebrows, Mason took a break and stepped back.

Although it looked more like a lumpy potato than the display bear, he'd done okay so far. Good enough to sell at The Bouche Gallery right now, he joked to himself. The autumn evening pressed, but he wanted to finish so he could show Beth.

In the end, the bear's forelegs looked kind of like wings pressed against the body. The toothless, oversized mouth was more of a yawn than a snarl. And the head, well it could be fixed with a little off here and there. Better. Not perfect, maybe a little too small now, but it passed for a first time. One leg turned out thicker than the other, but it gave the bear a comic character. Mason stepped back. Did it look like a penguin? No, a bear. A silly, funny, lovable bear. Hey, it was folk art.

Aware that weariness could cause a slapdash finish, he paused to focus and slowly sliced through the trunk below his sculpture. It was getting dark, so he decided to pick up the firewood the next day. The finished sculpture, stand included, was about three-feet tall and weighed a lot more than a mail bag full of catalogs. Gingerly, he loaded it across the bench seat of his pick-up and headed for home.

"Hey Beth," he yelled as he banged the base of the bear against the metal storm door.

"What?" She answered sharply as if irritated by the racket. "Where've you been?" They met in the kitchen.

Mason thumped the bear down on the linoleum and rested a hand on its rough-cut head, like a proud father presenting his short-stop son.

"What is *that?*" She held an earring she was making, a dangle of dark beads.

"A bear. I carved it with my new chain saw."

She laughed. But it was not the laugh of appreciation he'd imagined. "A bear? Oh, Mason, that's really awful."

"It's not so bad." In the harsh light of the kitchen, perhaps it resembled a child's Play-Dough creation. Still, the form was bear-like if not clearly a bear.

"You meant it as a joke, right?"

"Well, kinda," he said. "I bought the saw to cut firewood, but–." He cut himself off with a sardonic laugh.

"Just don't throw out your mail bag."

"Well, I didn't exactly picture it in The Art Institute." They both laughed, and Mason sensed something of a union with her that he hadn't felt for months. "I got to thinking what you said about me not having any hobbies, so I made this for you."

"For me?"

"Yeah," he grinned.

"Mason, that's sweet in a high-school kind of way," she smirked, and in that instant he just didn't like Beth much, "but you can't take up an interest for somebody else. It has to be your interest."

"There's no pleasing you is there? I can't make you happy. All that crap about hobbies last night was a cover," he said. "You want out, but you don't have the guts to say it."

"It's not so simple." She put the earring on the counter.

"You want an artist or an executive. A mailman won't measure up."

"That's not it. I never said that."

"You don't have to. You've risen so far that I'm an embarrassment to you."

"Don't be melodramatic, Mason. We have grown apart, I won't deny it. But that doesn't mean—"

"I may be a boring mailman, but I'm no coward. I'm not afraid to be straight with you. But obviously you can't be straight with me." He squatted down to wrap his arms around his bear and hoist it up. Then he hauled it outside and placed it on the seat of his truck. Elizabeth watched him leave from the door. Was she laughing? Crying? Did it matter?

Under the light of a gibbous moon, Mason drove back out to Sycamore Hollow, past his cousin's house. Unsure what brought him back, he kept rolling down the leaf-covered lane, waiting for the reason to become clear. He replayed what had happened in the kitchen, slowing it down to absorb the details.

A year from now, Mason projected, Beth—no, Elizabeth—would be dating that son-of-a-bitch, and Mason would deliver love letters between them. Would it be different if Mason and Beth had decided to get married like most of their friends? Then it dawned on him that Beth and Gene Bouche might get married–and who but Mason would carry their wedding invitations all over town? Humiliating.

He parked near where he had carved the bear. Aiming the lights into the woods, he left the engine idling and dragged the bear out, letting it fall to the ground with a thud. For a moment he looked at his rough–cut creation and recognized it as a pathetic attempt to keep her. He prepared to cut the bear to pieces, but noticed another tree, a dead shagbark hickory. As he pondered it, he envisioned a squirrel, sitting up with a hickory nut in its paws and its plume of a tail curled up its back.

Exactly as he'd done for the bear, he cut down the tree at chest height, letting the sawdust shower over him. It was difficult to carve with just the truck's headlights, so he got the small flashlight out of the glovebox. He felt like an idiot, but if he held the light in his teeth, he could see what he was doing. The squirrel was more challenging because he had to create it from imagination, but that made it more fun too. His shoulders ached from the weight of the saw and teeth hurt from clenching the light, but he kept at it. Sweat greased the folds of his neck, his elbows, his underarms. It was hard work, but a pleasure. He reserved judgment, and then he stepped back to give himself an honest assessment. It sucked. A little better than the bear, but it still sucked. He didn't care.

He stepped up, pressing the saw down against the wood.

Then it slipped. The saw slipped.

And it dove into Mason's left thigh, ripping a gash as long as his shoe, exposing for an instant the white bone before it gushed red. He threw the saw aside. He knew he was in trouble. If he dragged himself to the pick–up, he could get to a doctor. Oh God, it's bleeding like crazy, he thought. And the left leg of his gray uniform was burgundy in seconds, but it didn't feel wet because of the thick, warm blood. He recalled how Beth, like a worried mother, had feared a chain saw accident and made him promise never to use one alone. He dragged himself through the leaves–it hurt–grabbing handfuls of undergrowth to help pull. Pushing–Christ it hurt–with his right leg. He breathed hard. He felt his heart pounding and knew it was pumping the life out of him. Exhausted and dizzy, he felt less pain. Hurry up, he drove himself, can't stop. He saw the edge of the woods. He fought to remain conscious. Finally he pulled himself free of the trees. Only twenty feet to the truck. You won't have the strength to climb up or drive, he told himself. "Just get there," he ordered aloud.

He wondered if his life would pass before his eyes. Then he put his head down in the grass and laughed a little at what his friends would think of his bear, his squirrel. Then, as the match glow of his life dimmed into smoke, more than anything Mason wanted to lay his head in Beth's lap and have her stroke his hair.

Same as I Got

Chuck felt his father elbow him awake again and absorbed the stern look that said, 'Stay alert, boy,' but in the pre-dawn chill Chuck's mind kept drifting to the warm flannel sheets of his bed two miles away. He studied the edge of the woods where trees met the corn stubble and scanned the row of corn his father had left standing in the field to attract deer. Everything in shades of gray. Upwind of the woods and the corn, they sat in a deer blind his father had built at the base of a tree in an overgrown fence row. Chuck shifted on the green wool Army blanket–spread over tree roots that felt like antlers under him–and pulled the fleece collar up around his neck. He loved fishing, loved nature, and last night Chuck couldn't wait to go on his first deer hunt with his father, but now he imagined his fourth-grade friends asleep under blankets and remembered the heated truck his father had parked about a half-mile away when it still felt like midnight. Then they had walked down the tree-lined lane and across the field–the ground frozen enough to support his boots in the mud for a moment before they sank into the earth.

His father pulled a red plastic cup from his pocket and ran a big, dark thumb around the inside to clean out dirt and poured his son a cup of steaming coffee from the red and black buffalo-plaid thermos.

The cup warmed Chuck's cold fingers for the first time since they'd left home. Dad motioned for him to drink it, and Chuck lifted it to his nose. It smelled awful. When his lips broke the black-mirror surface, the bitterness made him close one eye and tongue his teeth. Dad grinned and gave him a nod and wink that he understood to mean we-men-are-in-this-together. Still, he hated the taste of coffee. But it was hot, so he took another sip, this one audible, and his father's small brown eyes snapped on him. Chuck withdrew into his coat for violating the absolute decree for silence. His father looked up, cupping his mouth with one hand, jaw muscles flexing, and drew it down over his jaw the color of a gun barrel with the new beard.

Men in the family and their deer-hunting friends shared a tradition of no shaving from a day before deer season. Their rule said you didn't shave until you bagged a buck. So Chuck had felt a little ashamed of his bearded Uncle Ron last year. Although Chuck's father had taken a good eight-point buck on opening day, he'd decided to keep his beard until Chuck had a kill. Now ten-year-old Chuck was ready for his first deer hunt with his father.

A few nights before, Chuck had eavesdropped on his Uncle Ron and his father discussing this deer hunt. He'd heard Ron, the younger of the two and unmarried, try to talk Ray out of it, asking him to lighten up on the boy and wait a couple of years, reminding Ray of his first hunt at the same age with their father. When

Chuck's father said the boy was ready, Chuck felt proud. But when he told Ron it wasn't easy to start forging a man out of a boy, it confused the ten-year-old.

Chuck thumbed the safety on top of his single-shot twenty gauge, the bluing almost completely worn off, so the barrel was the color of the lead deer slug inside. Then he looked at his father's pump-action twelve-gauge.

Chuck felt his father's elbow again and looked up quick to show he wasn't asleep, but Ray's small, dark eyes were trained on the woods. Chuck tried to trace them. Although it was lighter, the sun wasn't up, and a fog hung in the trees close to Owl Creek. Slower than he'd ever seen anyone move, Chuck watched his father's large, thick hands put down his coffee. A hand reached Chuck's leg, giving him the thumbs up, and then a heavy finger pointed toward the trees. Squinting and opening his eyes, Chuck saw nothing. Which branches were antlers? Which saplings were legs? His heart pounded. But he saw no horizontal lines, no flick of an ear, no patch of white, no black nose or glossy dark eye, no movement—none of the signs his father had taught him to look for. Then he felt his father's hand signal: one finger, no two, then a hole like holding an invisible pipe, then a flat hand turned over twice—it made Chuck think of a fish flopping on the bank—then the hole again, then three fingers and again the hole. Chuck studied the trees and looked back to the thick hand when it moved. He saw nothing. Where were they? He couldn't remember what the hand signals meant. Three does?

Then a doe materialized at the edge of the field not fifty yards away, tail twitching, nose in the air, and ears up like radar scanning. She was beautiful in her gray winter coat, more beautiful than the photos he'd seen in the pages of *Field & Stream*. Chuck thought his heart, pumping like the engine of his granddad's diesel tractor, would give them away. Second and third does stepped into the corn stubble and conducted the same twitching, sniffing, listening search while the first nosed the ground for corn. Chuck's hands began to shake, so he squeezed the gun tighter. The three deer inched–step scan, step scan–toward the strip of corn.

One doe looked over her back toward the woods, and the big hand opened wide all five fingers on Chuck's thigh. A buck. And Chuck saw him just before he emerged from the trees. White breath rose from the buck's black nostrils. The eight–point antlers– nature's crown for a king of the woods, Chuck thought–were slick and sharp, white on the ends, dark and nubby like a tree branch down by the cautious, flicking ears. The buck sprang into the open- ing, floating with the bushy white tail held high. Transfixed by the buck's splendor, Chuck had to be elbowed to shoulder the single- shot twenty–gauge. It felt heavy and shook in his hands. His breath became short and choppy like stuttering. Don't belly shoot, he re- membered, hit shoulder or neck. But the image of his lead slug ripping through the flawless gray neck or sleek, muscular shoul- der, held him. From the corner of his blurred eye, he saw his father shoulder his shotgun to back him up.

Ray finally whispered in a stern voice, "Shoot, boy."

The buck's head jerked their way, ears spread wide, and with- out aiming Chuck yanked the trigger, and the twenty–gauge kicked his shoulder and jaw hard because he hadn't cheeked–down on the stock like he'd been taught. Instantly, he heard the KAWOG, snap, KAWOG, snap, KAWOG, snap of his father's big twelve- gauge pump.

Leaving his gun, Chuck's shaky legs could hardly run after Ray's broad, lumbering back striding for the downed buck. When Chuck caught up, he saw the huge black boot pressing one antler into the soft earth. Blood trickled from the buck's quivering nostrils. "Cut his throat," Ray ordered.

Chuck stared at the beautiful buck, the gray winter coat, the white patch on his neck, the deep blackness of its wild eyes flash- ing full of fear, then up to his father's small, dark eyes and black bearded face twisted in anger. "Cut his damn throat."

Chuck froze.

"Then shoot him," Ray said shoving the twelve-gauge at Chuck. But the boy's hands didn't come up to take the shotgun. The big voice boomed in his face, "Then hold it! Hold my gun, boy!" And a hand reached out weakly to take the warm, black barrel.

Muttering about a poor excuse for a son, Ray took out his knife and slit the buck's throat. A short squeal and blood gushed over Chuck's boots. He jumped back and the steaming blood filled the depression his boots had made in the mud. Chuck's throat tightened and tears spilled before he could check it. "What's the matter with you?" Ray yelled. "You seen me bleed hogs. This ain't no different."

But to Chuck it couldn't have been more different—the filthy smelling, grunting hogs compared to nature's crowned king. "I won't have no crybaby for a son. Now get out your knife and help me field dress this buck."

Still Chuck couldn't move, couldn't follow orders.

"Give me your tag," Ray demanded, his voice spitting disgust.

"But, I missed. You shot him."

Ray slapped his son hard across the ear, knocking him to the ground and snatched him up by the coat, bringing him close to the red mouth and coffee breath surrounded by the gun-barrel-dark beard. "This is your first buck. Same as I got my first. Now give me your damn tag." Ray pulled at the boy's coat pocket for the deer tag, "Wait in the truck." Chuck didn't move. "GET!" Chuck jerked to his feet and sprinted away from his father and away from the truck into the woods along Owl Creek in the direction that the deer had come.

*

Ray watched his son flee and remembered his own first buck. His trembling ten-year-old arms had missed a forkhorn at the salt lick, and his father, firing at almost the same instant, downed the young buck in a clean kill. He'd hung back when his old man bled the animal. Then he handed young Ray the knife and told him to gut the forkhorn. When he hesitated, his father cuffed him and said a hunter cleans his own kill so get to it. Ray slit open the warm body and pulled out the steaming entrails while his father sat at the base of a tree, rolling a smoke (bloodstains on the cigarette paper). "Save the heart and liver," his old man ordered. That night his mother boiled the heart and the old man made Ray sit down and together they ate the gray heart muscle of his first buck.

He was a hard man, Ray's father, harder than Ray. In Chuck, who had just vanished into the woods at the edge of the field, Ray saw something of himself, a soft, unacceptable side that didn't serve a man well. Toward his own father, he had felt an emotional amalgam of hate, fear, and respect. Ray had been annealed against the cold, hard man. And now, though it pained him, he felt he had to do the same for Chuck.

Had his own father hesitated in his harsh treatment? If so, Ray never saw any indication. It was not easy to be hard. Part of him admired Chuck for running, for the courage to run. Ray squatted down to dress the buck, but when he lifted the warm heart, he tossed it aside.

The Fires of Youth

Sometimes Jack hated them, and finally they were gone. Like a jail door sliding open to release him, the blue Dodge curved down the sand and red clay lane. It bumped across the bridge made of old telephone poles and rolled out of sight. His parents, two kid brothers, and little sister were headed for Rankelwood, Kentucky to visit his grandmother. A whole weekend of freedom. Jack ran inside the turquoise-and-white mobile home to call his best friend C.J.

As he dialed, he wished Julie were still around and imagined having her spend the night, so he could hold her and comfort her. They'd talked about spending a night together somehow, dreamed about it, but it never happened. Probably never would now. For a day he'd carried Julie's letter in his hip pocket, trying to decide what to do and knowing he had to do something.

C.J. answered the phone.

"They're gone," Jack said. "Let's raise some hell tonight, man."

Taking the old Ford pickup which was a dull black color except for one red fender, they drove from Nema to Bloomington where they paid a 21-year-old college guy five bucks to buy them a case of Budweiser and a bottle of Jack Daniels. They popped their first cans as they raced back to Nema, crossing the double yellow line on blind curves, Marlboros hung from the corner of their mouths. They tossed their first empties out the window. For some reason it felt good to deliberately litter with a beer can and to watch in the side mirror as the can tumbled on the blacktop until it sprang into the roadside weeds. When he turned off State Road 64, the truck fishtailed in the gravel, limestone dust rising like smoke. Then, steering into their lane, the pickup slammed over the telephone pole bridge, and rattled up the hill to the mobile home. Jack took the three steps in one bound while C.J. stopped to water the lawn.

Inside, it felt big and quiet, so Jack clicked on the radio and switched from *Country 101* to *The Rock of Southern Indiana* and turned it up loud. His mother wouldn't stand for it. But she couldn't hear it from Kentucky. C.J. came in, took the cigarette from his mouth, and pumped both fists in the air, yelling as loud and long as he could "YEAAAAHH." Then they both whooped and jumped around the living room like a pair of wild men, "Wo, wo, woooo." The mobile home shook under them until they threw themselves, C.J. onto the flowered couch, Jack into the vinyl La-Z-Boy recliner. They popped open their second Buds and downed the beer, pausing to "aaahh" at the satisfaction, pretending they enjoyed the taste more than they did, more than Mountain Dew, or Dr. Pepper. C.J. got up and turned on the TV. Jack clicked off the radio. Nothing on the boob tube except the last half of *Bullet*.

Jack pointed to the screen and said, "Didja know Steve Mc-

Queen's from Indiana?"

"Didja know you tell me that every time you see his face?" C.J. answered.

"That's 'cause I know how dumb you are. Can't remember a thing," Jack said.

"I remember you're 'bout as weak as my little sister."

When Jack finished his third beer, he flicked on the radio again. C.J. put his cigarette in the ash tray molded in the shape of Kentucky and got up to turn off the TV. But Jack attacked before C.J. reached the box, bringing him down on the narrow strip of aqua-blue sculpted carpet. "I'll show you who's weak, you dumb ox," Jack said. They wrestled between the blaring radio and the TV, knocked into the coffee table, and kicked the particle-board paneling. Jack was mean and tough as barb wire, but he gave up twenty-five pounds and three inches to C.J. who also had an extraordinary tolerance for pain and seemed to take a weird pleasure in it. Soon size won over quickness as C.J. pinned Jack and sat on his chest.

"Get off me, you big homo," Jack said.

C.J. hauled himself up.

Jack said, "Let's get out of here."

"Where to?"

"I don't know, man, let's just go."

Tonight, for Julie, he would right things with Henshaw, but he wasn't ready to tell C.J. about it. "Let's find some girls or somethin'. Raise a little hell."

They took the beer and Jack Daniels along. Outside, Jack imagined a video of himself as he leaned against the red fender and lit a cigarette, the match flashed something wild in his face, and he stuffed the pack in the pocket of his flannel shirt. Feeling the first beers, he opened a fourth and climbed into the pickup. C.J. did the same. They cruised by the high school and saw a few football jerks hanging around. They drove to Dairy Queen, C.J. saying he wanted to find Lena Bates or some of the other hot girls, saying that's what Jack needed to get over Julie. But they saw only three of the popular girls in the junior class and didn't even bother stopping to talk. As far as Jack was concerned, those girls may as well have been on a TV screen. It didn't matter anyway, he and Julie didn't even have time to decide if they should break up over her family's sudden move away or try to stay together. Jack's first and only real girlfriend gone just like that.

They left the DQ and roamed around Nema. "Jack and C.J., two studs cruising 'round town," C.J. said and finally lit the cigarette that had dangled from his mouth for several minutes. Jack noted that C.J. held the match the way he often did until the flame crept up and burned his finger tips. Then he flicked it out the window.

Beyond town on State Road 196, they circled back toward Nema through the country roads. The truck's lights flickered against tree trunks in woodlots and waved over moonlit gray fields. They passed a few spots where Jack and Julie used to go parking, steaming up the windows of his parents' Dodge or of this Ford pickup. As the truck neared the farm where Julie had lived, C.J. leaned out the window and threw a beer can against a one-lane-bridge sign with a bang like a shotgun blast that interrupted the night's quiet and Jack's musings.

Jack stopped his father's black pickup with the one red fender in front of the "For Rent" sign at the vacant farmhouse where Julie had lived. "Wonder what Julie's doing tonight."

"Her dad got a job at a steel mill in Gary, or Hammond, or somewheres up north, right?" C.J. said.

"He's lookin'," Jack answered as he studied the old white farmhouse with a green roof and a recently broken window. "I miss Jewels," he said and realized he'd opened himself up for teasing. But C.J. let it pass.

"You ever write to her?"

With his friend's words, he felt the letter in his back pocket and responded to it and not his friend. "She hated Old Man Henshaw."

"You two ever talk on the phone?"

He hadn't called her since the seven-page letter because he didn't know what to say. "Got a letter from her yesterday. She told how Henshaw was always givin' her these looks. And how he used to walk in their house without knockin' to hassle her dad about the farm. Then one night–"

"But it's Henshaw's house, right?" C.J. asked.

Jack couldn't believe his ears and his look must have said enough because C.J. shut up and turned to his window, facing the corn stubble, gray in the moonlight. Jack focused once more on Julie's house. In a few seconds, C.J. went on, "I always liked Julie's dad. I'da baled his hay for nothin'." He laughed and added, "Course nothin' is 'bout what we got paid."

Jack looked at C.J. again. "We was workin' for Henshaw even then. Whose hay did you think we was puttin' up? CJ, sometimes you're dumb as a hard-on. Besides, Henshaw don't pay us much more now, and he's rich."

"Yeah, you're right," C.J. said. "Here, man, have a beer."

*

Instead of taking the beer, Jack backed the truck up and, with a bark of worn Goodyears on the tarred road, he turned around and headed for Henshaw's home place.

"Where we goin'?" C.J. asked.

"Piss on Henshaw," Jack answered.

"Whatever, man," C.J. said and handed him the Jack Daniels.

Old man Henshaw operated the largest farm in the county, a mix of cattle and crops, on six different farms where tenant farmers like Julie's folks did all the work while Henshaw drove around in a big Buick, collecting his money. As he neared the Henshaw place, Jack turned off the lights and cut the engine, coasting to a stop at the edge of a copse near the barn and out of the sight-line from Henshaw's house.

Jack took the empty beer cans and hurled them out into the barn lot, then climbed the fence, unzipped his fly, and watered Henshaw's gray siding, shuffling sideways along the wall, making an erratic horizontal line. C.J. laughed and got out of the truck to follow his buddy's example.

"C'mon," Jack said and pushed open the sliding door a bit, and squeezed into the smell of aged manure and dry clover hay. He stood at the door, half-swallowed by the dark interior of the barn. Somehow he was going to make this S.O.B. pay.

C.J. ran through the moonlight to the truck to get the beer and bottle of Jack Daniels. The flashlight stuck magnetically to the metal dash glowed weak as a match when he checked it, but he brought it anyway. Jack went ahead into the barn confounded by the cave-like blackness inside. Blindly he groped for the ladder to the hay-mow and started up.

"Where are you?" C.J. whispered.

"Up here," Jack said and saw the dull glow of the flashlight illuminate his pumpkin-colored workshoes. He stepped into the loft, imagining his shoes disappearing from C.J.'s vision into the black hole. He climbed up blocks of hay, ascending through bars of smoky moonlight that slipped around the loose siding, and opened the high hay doors. They let in a purple pentagon of moonlight which broke across the blocks of hay.

Below, with the flashlight's filament burning like an ember, C.J. appeared to be floating. "Don't let that beer get warm, boy," Jack said and scrambled down monkey-quick but out of control, landing on a level of bales, and they both laughed.

They sat on the bales they had stacked the previous summer for Henshaw and took turns drawing off the bottle of bitter-hot Jack Daniels and chasing it with slugs of beer. Their eyes adjusted to the scant light.

C.J. rambled on about the car he was rebuilding, a 1976 Dodge Charger. A heap, but he was sure it would be the hottest wheels in town if he ever got it fixed.

Jack hardly listened, thinking about Julie and settling the score with Henshaw.

"So whaddaya think?" C.J. asked.

"Huh?"

"What's with you, man?"

"Got a lot on my mind. Let's just sit here and not talk for a bit."

"Sure. I just wondered if you thought I should put glasspacks on my car."

"That'd be great. Can we just be quiet for a minute?"

"Okay by me, big thinker."

In his head, Jack replayed the scene in the letter from Jewels:

One night Henshaw walks in while Julie's folks and brother are gone and she's on the couch watching TV in a flannel night gown. No robe or nothing. She grabs for the ugly orange and brown knitted comforter hung over the back. But the couch is shoved against the wall, so she cain't get it. Henshaw asks if her folks is home. She says no, hoping he'll leave. But he don't. He comes over and sits next to her, looking her up and down. Then Henshaw starts in talking how things are rough for her daddy and how she can make things easier. And he reaches out a filthy, stinking hand and touches her small ankle and up her calf. She pulls her feet away, and tries to get up, but he grabs her, his claws all over her body, reachin' up her nightie, tearing at her panties, and laughing while she fights. She breaks away and locks herself in the bathroom. The disgusting old bastard tries to talk her out, saying it's gonna be trouble for her daddy if she don't come out. But she don't. Then he goes, 'Folks in town will think you're a whore if you tell. A girl sitting around near naked while her momma and daddy are gone and with a man in the house.' For saying that alone, Jack would like to bust that old man's face, let alone all the rest. He can feel his heart rushing while he lays on the hay as if he'd just sprinted a hundred yards. Julie stayed locked in the bathroom till her mom and dad got home. But she never told anybody until she told Jack in yesterday's letter. Jack cried when he read it, cried for the pain it had caused Julie, for his own shame at failing to protect her the way a man should protect his girl, and for the anger and frustration he felt toward Henshaw for making Julie's family move away about a month after that bastard touched her. And now she blamed herself for the trouble on her family and the pain she brought upon Jack.

He didn't know what to do. But he knew he had to do something.

Jack took a long drink off the bottle, feeling the whisky burn. Then another. He'd like to sneak up and jab a big knife into that shitbag Henshaw. Again and again, jab, jab, jab. Jack spat into the hay.

"What's the matter with you?" C.J. said. "Panting and spitting, you ain't gonna puke are ya?"

"Ain't gonna puke."

"Well, you're panting like a big dog."

"You practicin' to be somebody's nurse?"

"You practicin' to be somebody's coon hound?"

They both laughed at that. Jack drained his beer can and threw the red and white cylinder into the darkness of the hayloft, and it disappeared without a sound. C.J. stood up and rifled his, and it too disappeared into the black almost as it left his hand and landed somewhere soundlessly. Jack wondered at the depth of the quiet.

With camaraderie renewed, they passed the whiskey back and fourth. Then C.J. farted, and the two boys burst into laughter. "You pig!" Jack said, and both haw-hawed louder and harder than either thought it was funny. Lifted by the alcohol, laughter caught on the laughter, until it was a breathless, stomach cramper. They rolled on the hay bales knocking mindlessly into each other. C.J. pushed Jack off one level of hay bales on to the next, and he rolled down to the next like falling down giant grass stairs and giggling all the harder at it.

"I hear you can light them," C.J. snickered. "Ever light a fart?"

Wiping his eyes, Jack answered, "No, but if anyone can, you're the man."

"Got that right," C.J. said. "Well, here goes."

"Better be a fast one, or you'll blow up," Jack said. And they both went through another laughing spell. C.J. sat back with his feet up in the air, lit a match at the crotch of his jeans, and–poof– a blue flame flashed off his ass like a gas stove lighting and going out instantly. Both boys screamed with laughter–their mouths open wide as a largemouth bass, tears flowing from their eyes, and pounding the hay, raising an awful dust that choked them so they laughed and coughed at once. They washed down the dust with gulps of whiskey.

"Let's burn it," Jack said in a complete monotone.

C.J. stopped laughing, sobered by Jack's tone. "What?"

"The barn, man, let's burn the fucker." He turned to C.J.'s face, blank as a freshly washed chalk board. "It's Henshaw's. Let's burn the shitbag's barn. Let's burn it, man. We'll show that son-of-a-bitch. Let's burn his barn to the ground!"

By the time C.J. nodded, Jack was already lighting the hay.

They swarmed around with matches igniting the dry hay and flipping burning matches in flaming arcs. Jack paused in the yellow light as the sound like that of a distant jet rose up all around them. C.J. stopped too, and they spun on their knees to see the fire spreading fast in the dry hay.

"Let's go!" C.J. screamed. But the openings in the flames swept shut in a horrific, hungry roar. They grabbed at each other and looked up at the hay doors, now a pentagon of darkness. Even if they could beat the racing flames, it would be 30 feet to the ground. Unspoken understanding sent Jack diving into the fire, C.J. right behind him, flannel shirts pulled over their heads, diving for the dark square in the haymow floor, diving as skin burned and exposed hair singed. They fell through the black hole about nine feet onto the hard dirt floor.

Scrambling to their feet, the boys rushed through the dark barn with the sound of the fire snapping, whooshing above them– rushed, stumbling out into the moonlight, wild and blinded as frightened horses with the smell of smoke and death in their flaring nostrils. C.J. ran for the black pickup, but Jack went the other way, hefting a rock and heaving it through an upstairs window of Henshaw's big brick farmhouse. And he stood there. A dog began barking.

"Come on, man," C.J. yelled, "let's get the hell out of here."

Curtains moved at another window and soon the old man appeared at the front door with a shotgun. His white hair stood a muss like a swirl of smoke on his head.

"Come on," C.J. said.

Jack stood.

"I know who you are," old man Henshaw called from the porch.

"I know who you are too," Jack answered. He saw the old woman appear at the broken window. Plenty loud for both of them to hear he hollered, "And I know what you are. I know what you did to that girl and why you made her family move."

Jack stood for a moment longer, then turned and walked toward the truck. Flames glowed through the cracks in the siding, and smoke boiled from the open doors at the top of the hayloft. In the moonlight, the smoke was pretty, pretty as a knee–length skirt billowing around the legs of a running girl, Julie running out from school to the parking lot to catch a ride with him.

When Jack got in the truck and started it, C.J. said "You crazy? He probably saw you."

"He saw me all right, but he ain't gonna do nothin' about it."

Jack got in the truck and watched the fire. "That'll show the old bastard," he said, but he didn't believe it. He felt no satisfaction in striking a blow for justice, for Julie. Even if he burned all of Henshaw's barns, killed some of his cattle, or sabotaged his equipment, none of it would bring her back.

He watched the smoke billowing from the barn like rage. Smoke trailing away, thinning as it went. Smoke vanishing in the night sky.

Wins and Losses

Tommy White was a member of the Sassafras County High School class of 1966 with 66 students—a miracle folks in Nema said—and that miracle was backed by a more important one: the Mountaineers had a good basketball team. The best in 25 years. Tommy, a lean but broad six-foot-two-inch forward, started every game. And the Mountaineers beat the big schools in south-central Indiana: Bloomington, Bedford, Martinsville, and Columbus.

On March 6th, the night of the sectional finals, the team bus pulled out of the school parking lot, and Tommy turned, craning his long neck, to marvel at the line of eight school buses and string of headlights from cars following them from Nema to the cavernous gym in Seymour. The light from the headlights made deep shadows on his angular face; that, combined with the contrast of his dark hair and pale skin, gave him the look of a black and white movie caught in time. Tom couldn't help but wonder, regretting the thought even as it dawned on him, if all those people would follow the team home if they lost to highly touted Seymour as they had so many times before.

Tommy was the third-best player on the team, but on this night, the game slowed down—the ball floated in slow motion for him. He saw every seam, could read Wilson Official as his hands reached out for a pass or rebound. He squared his large elbows and knees to fend off opponents. Without thought his body sprang out, diving to claim loose balls, and his hands ripped the orange from opponents. Still, the Mountaineers trailed Seymour in the fourth quarter, and then Tommy White found a reserve of energy.

Relentlessly aggressive, he played the game of his life. In the fourth quarter alone, Tommy had seven rebounds, two steals, and ten points. And Sassafras County upset Seymour for the school's first Sectional Championship since before World War II.

After the game, a crowd of men, women, and kids turned out for a pep rally at the school, it felt like the whole town was there, and when they introduced Tommy White, he got the loudest cheer of all. After the rally, there was a big party at Janis Hollingsworth's and Tom White didn't have to ask for beer—people just put them in his hand and slapped him on the back. He must have gotten congratulations kisses from twenty girls, even Laura Dove. Tom noticed his quiet, homeroom friend Cindy Watt standing alone near the fireplace and brought her a can of Pepsi.

"Hi, how's my homeroom buddy?" With one hand, he offered her the drink and then gave her an easy, one-arm hug.

"Thank you," she said, taking the drink. He had to lean close, hardly able to hear her over party. She raised her chin toward his ear and added, "I'm fine. How are you after that big game?"

"I'm great," he yelled. "That was so much fun, winning the sectional like that." He leaned in again to catch any response.

"I bet," she said. "You're amazing."

That's what he thought she said. But before he could ask, one of the guys pulled him away and a bunch of boys cleared the furniture out of the living room and the whole party counted as several boys, including Tom, started a one-clap push-up contest on the blue shag carpet. When it got down to Tom White and Steve Babcock all the other guys jumped on them. The heap of high school boys tangled themselves into a wrestling knot of screaming laughter. Cindy had receded to the back of the crowd against the wall but was smiling at the silly energy. When it broke up, everyone bounced and shook in ecstatic dance to loud music, shouting, "Sectional Champs, Sectional Champs," so when the record skipped no one even noticed.

The wildly jubilant party continued until some "Seymorons" in their Seymour High letter jackets showed up outside. They'd been racing up and down the street in a hopped-up, green GTO. Screeching tires filled the air with the smell of burned rubber.

The GTO skidded to a stop and the doors flung open spilling five boys and empty beer cans into the street. "Where's Lily White?" they yelled.

Janis Hollingsworth started to call the sheriff, but one of the boys said, "We don't need no cops to fight for us." So Tom, Steve Babcock, and two other boys went out while the rest of the party gathered on the front porch and at the windows.

"We kicked your butts on the basketball court," one boy said. "Now you Seymorons want your butts kicked again?"

"Try it, hillbilly. Just try it," said the driver of the GTO, the smallest and cockiest of the Seymorons.

"Gritty midget," Babcock spat and shoved the little loudmouth. Then one of the basketball players from Seymour shoved Babcock against a parked car. Tom White snapped a half nelson on the Seymour basketball player and, sensing his balance shift, flung him to the pavement. Meanwhile the other boys squared off, cursing each other and threatening to bust each other's heads.

Steve Babcock–the biggest and most athletic of all the boys–stood squarely, silently, with fists tight and heavy as shot puts, his jaw flexing and relaxing as his eyes snapped from one Seymour boy to another, but none of them looked at Babcock's face.

As Tom White faced the boy he'd thrown to the ground, the little cocky kid shoved him from behind. Tom turned, "You little chickenshit."

Then sprinting to his GTO, the small kid came back with a pump–action shotgun pointed at Tommy White.

Tom held out both palms, "Easy, Man."

"What's the matter Lily White?" He laughed, "Big shot scared of a little buckshot?"

Another Seymour boy grabbed the shotgun and pumped it to show Tom it was empty.

"You little chickenshit," Tom started forward again, but Babcock held him back.

"I'll show you who's a chicken. You got a car Lily White?"

"I got a car." Tom said and pointed to his dad's four-door Chevy.

"Where's the horse?" The little guy laughed. "Ever play chicken, Lily White?"

*

Out on State Road 64 where it's straight and flat, between Nema and Columbus, out near Clay Flats, four Seymorons got out of the GTO and waited at the bridge over the West Fork of Owl Creek. The GTO turned back toward the party house about a half mile away. When its lights flashed, they were to go–Tommy in his father's Chevy and the little guy from Seymore in the GTO. More than twenty kids crowded around Tom's car, others, more cautious, tried to watch from the windows of the Hollingsworth house.

"Show 'em what we're made of in Nema, Tommy," one boy said. Then Steve Babcock leaned in the driver's window and said, "When you get close, keep speed and close your eyes. That coward will chicken out."

Tom realized how stupid this was. But it had gone too far to turn back. He watched the GTO's lights, but they didn't flash. And he hoped they wouldn't. He hoped someone would say, 'This is nuts, Tom. Let's go.' But the kids screamed toward the bridge, "You chickens. Chickens!"

Tom glanced out the window and saw the worried eyes of his quiet friend Cindy Watt who stood with her hands folded before her. Only she was in focus, fixed and crisp while the rest of the party crew jeered toward the bridge: "You chickens! Chickens."

And then the lights flashed, and everyone cheered, and Tom floored the Chevy, aiming it at the GTO's headlights.

When they got close, Tom White eased right, into his lane, closed his eyes, and stayed on the gas. Then he got scared and looked. But it was too late. The GTO's lights were right there, moving in slow motion as the ball had during game. The lights hung there very close, and he saw the face of the boy from Seymour screaming, and then the lights disappeared. The clack of bumpers and popping headlights, the groan of wrinkling metal, and Tommy slid forward on the seat for a long time. Then the abrupt impact against the steering wheel, the final jamming leap of car against car, and he felt cubes of safety glass in his mouth.

Then it was quiet except for a strange sound that Tommy White had never heard before, something like the sound of rain falling on a blanket.

*

When the 65 gowned and mortarboarded graduates of 1966 filed into the gymnasium three months later, Cindy Watt felt everyone look at her, and she felt deeply alone being last in line. She walked behind her friend Meg Watson. From first grade on, she and Tom White and Meg Watson had been at the end of class lines together–Tom right behind her or beside her, Meg in front or to the other side. Her book ends. Home room, yearbook photos, small-pox vaccines. Cindy concentrated on the back of Meg Watson's white gown with emerald–green trim and on her swinging black hair. She wished Meg were taller. When Meg waved to someone, Cindy thought, "Please don't do that. People will look at us."

Cindy had worked on the decoration committee. From the Methodist Church they'd borrowed the red carpet for the center aisle. From Berry Hill Nursing Home came the two large, musty-smelling ferns on stands at the end of the center aisle, which obstructed the view for several graduates. The First Presbyterian Church had loaned their ornate walnut altar as a podium. And the school secretary had arranged for the fifteen-foot-long American flag from Patch Ford to be hung behind the speaker's platform, to conceal the scoreboard. Nema Furniture had sent eight Naugahyde wing chairs for the stage, and all eight were positioned (though only six were needed). And the white folding chairs had come from Columbus Rent-All.

As soon as Cindy Watt sat next to Tommy White's empty chair, she began to cry. Someone had accidentally rented and set up 66 white folding chairs. Cindy had always had a crush on Tom White, more than a crush. She looked down at the white legs of the chair in front of her so her mousy-brown hair hung down around her face to hide her tears. Meg handed her a Kleenex and squeezed her hand. Cindy Watt didn't hear the commencement address or the student speeches that rang of the past and the future for the class of 1966. Coach McCord said a few words about Tom White and asked for a moment of silence in his memory. It was a silence punctuated by sniffles around the gym.

Rather than listen to the speakers, Cindy Watt remembered how Tom always said, "Hi Cindy," in the halls. He was nice to her. Although Tom White was one of the most popular boys and she was practically invisible, they were friends. If she went to a party, and she rarely did, Tom always talked to her. Once Tom had said to two other popular boys, "You guys know Cindy Watt," and the boys said, "What? Cindy what again? What? What?" She felt stupid, and they'd laughed. Tom laughed too, then cupped her shoulder and whispered, "Don't let these goofballs get to you." Yes, he was her friend.

Cindy thought if she had said something out on the road that night when he looked at her, she might have stopped Tom. If she'd said, "Tom this is stupid. What does it prove? You don't need this," he would have listened. If for no other reason than that she rarely spoke, he would have listened.

She could have saved him. Should have saved him.

Meg Watson patted Cindy's leg. Cindy thought it was to comfort her. But then she realized her row was filing out to get diplomas. Walking up to the speaker's platform, Cindy wished she weren't at the end of the class, wished she weren't crying. She felt as if a huge, empty glass box followed her down the red carpet.

"Congratulations, Cindy," the principal said and handed her the roll of paper bound by a simple green ribbon. People had applauded at the end of each row, but silence followed Cindy as if all waited for Tom White. But Cindy Watt was last, the sixty–fifth graduate in the class of 1966. After a moment an applause took wing, but with little enthusiasm.

The last of the 65 Sassafras County High School graduates made their way to their seats. Again Cindy Watt felt the void behind her where her friend Tom White should have been. She tried once more to hide her tears. Cindy passed her chair and sat on Tommy White's. Meg patted Cindy's chair and whispered, "This is your seat." But Cindy stayed in Tommy White's chair, pressing herself down and back into the chair.

The Thing She Saw

"It's Cold, O'Pap. My word it's cold, and that wind," Rebecca White whispered to her grandfather. Always whispering because she didn't want the family to hear and think she was crazy for speaking to someone who'd died over twenty years ago. Nickel nosed the door open and came in to see her, his whip of a tail wagging. The pointer was ghost–like in his white–and–brown coat and pale golden eyes. "You silly dog," Rebecca said and held out her hand. The twelve–year–old dog had begun to answer to the name O'Pap. Nickel licked her hand, and she scratched behind his ears and strained from the hospital bed to see out the window, just an arched bit of clear glass surrounded by the abstract magic of Jack

Frost. "Like you used to say, it's the kind of cold," she whispered, "that makes chickens brittle."

She watched the snow blow. "I bet John went to school without a hat, O'Pap, and that boy had a basketball game too. He'll go out with a wet head and come home with ice in his hair."

Never far from her thoughts, Rebecca spoke to O'Pap often in the last months as she lay in the rented hospital bed in Tommy's old room with the beige, baseball-player wall paper. Her grandfather had been a religious man, a stand-in preacher at Hill County churches, looking tall and broad up there before the flock. Quiet goodness and wisdom had run deep in her grandfather, a man with an eighth-grade education. More than any man she'd ever known, Rebecca White loved and admired O'Pap. In his time, there wasn't as much a man had to do maybe, but it seemed to Rebecca that he could do most everything. A farmer all his life–scratching out a living from the unyielding fields outside Nema–he also worked at the sawmill in Baileys Switch, was a volunteer fireman, and for many years drove a school bus. Whatever needed fixing, O'Pap could fix.

If he were alive maybe he could fix me, she thought.

Perhaps she thought of O'Pap because this cancer had made her old. Old like he was when on his death bed at eighty-seven, he'd said to her: "Don't cry, my darlin' Becky. We'll see each other again in the house of the Lord. I'll meet you at the gate to lead you in. And it won't be long really. Oh, you'll live a long, full life just like me, but a lifetime is just a blink of the eye to Heaven's clock." That was the last time she saw him. He died on the coldest night of the year, and next to Tommy's untimely death in a car crash, it was her greatest loss. Since the night O'Pap died Rebecca had carried a dull ache, like an open space, deep inside. Tommy had been a first grader then, and Gail a toddler, Johnny not even born.

Last summer and fall she'd thought she would die on a cold November or December night like her grandfather had, and never see the New Year, but she'd made it and reached her 48th birthday. And she felt stronger now even if she didn't look it. Perhaps O'Pap was right, she might live a long life yet. But now she was concerned with living long enough to see John graduate from high school in June. And she'd love to watch him play football and graduate from Butler University. He'd be the first child on either side to graduate from college. But she'd be grateful to see June.

When she pulled herself out of bed, something she hadn't been able to do in September, her translucent feet cracked on the cold, wood floor. At the window, she watched snow swirl around the neighbor's tinseled Christmas tree set out on the snow for the trash. She thought, they know the trash men will leave that sit. Every year they put their tree out, and every year the trash men leave it, and it ends up at the edge of the field behind our house where I'll look out the kitchen window and catch a glint of sunlight off the tinsel and make John, when he got home from school, drag the Christmas carcass to our trash barrel and burn it.

Then the wind gusted, making the storm window rattle and lifting a layer of snow like a sheet on a clothesline, and the neighbor's Christmas tree came to life. The wind lifted it upright on its stump for an instant and blew it over the snowbank into the street. Rebecca laughed and bent forward resting her hands on her knees. Nickel sniffed her behind, and she slapped his nose. He went over and laid down heavily on the braided rug as she watched the tree roll and tumble down the street, a Christmas dancer twirling off stage for another year.

When the tree had rolled out of sight, Rebecca White went downstairs, firmly gripping the rail with two hands and planting both feet on each step before lowering to the next. Nickel followed.

Waiting for the coffee to perk, she gravitated to the window. In the back yard, sparrows, wrens, and chickadees fought the frigid wind to flit between the bird feeder and her overgrown rose bush. Rebecca checked the thermometer Tommy had mounted outside the kitchen window for her years ago–five below zero.

Then Rebecca's eye was drawn by some gnostic force from the thermometer to focus on a figure in black standing in the snowy bean field beyond the yard. At first she thought it Lucille Mossman on one of her wanders. But the posture was wrong, tall and thin. It was a man, facing her. Judge Howe? No. Rebecca whispered, "O'Pap? Is it you?" She was not afraid–she was happy. And then she remembered–

The telephone rang, but Rebecca White didn't move. "Don't come now O'Pap. I got that boy to raise. I have to see John graduate and go off to college." The telephone rang. "I'm getting strong again. It may be the coldest day of the year," the telephone rang again, "but my spring is coming." She turned and snatched up the phone.

A slightly familiar, halting voice spoke: "Good morning, this is Cindy Watt, I was calling because I wanted to–."

"What?" Rebecca said trying to see out the window, but she couldn't.

"Yes Watt," the young woman's voice said, "Cindy Watt." Pause.

"I'm sorry," Rebecca said, "I don't know anyone named Cindy Watt. I'm afraid I can't talk right now. I'm very busy."

The young woman apologized quickly and hung up.

When Rebecca got back to the window, the numen had vanished. Nothing there but the snow blowing across the yard, and blowing across the field, and small birds flitting between the feeder and the rose bush.

Finding the Words

"Hey, Cooper, you want a ride to the Martinsville game?" Susan Patch says as she fills her chrome thermos with black coffee for work.

For as long as Cooper can remember, he and his mom have gone to basketball games together. "Can't tonight," the boy says, feeling his voice rise slightly as he rushes on, "I got to work at *The Note* after school. And then I got to study for a test."

"On what?"

"Shakespeare. *Julius Caesar.*"

"Shakespeare over basketball? You ain't getting soft on me are you?" Susan teases and twists the thermos cap down tight. She doesn't like the coffee at work, so she brings her own to the Patch

Ford dealership. Grandpa started the undersized business, and now she owns part of it with her two brothers, but they can't agree on coffee. Among other things.

"They're number five in the state, Mom. They're going to kill us." Cooper pours a bowl of Fruit Loops.

"Kyle Knox against Jerry Stokes," Susan says, "could be interesting."

Kyle again. Since Cooper got cut from the team, he doesn't see much of his old friend, and he doesn't feel as close to his mother. Weird how his mom likes basketball so much. She was the only girl in a family of basketball nuts, and she was a pretty good player. Cooper's dad never played. He left for Florida when Cooper was five, so he can hardly remember his father, and he doesn't bring him up to Mom. Still a sore subject.

"I'd like to go, Mom, but I can't." Cooper sits down at the kitchen table and starts shoveling in the cereal.

Susan pours Cooper a glass of orange juice and sets it beside him. "When you guys are seniors," Susan says as she zips her winter coat over her sport coat, "Kyle could carry your team as far as we went, maybe farther."

Cooper knows all about Super Sue's Southern-Indiana Regional Champion team. While working as a copy boy at *The Nema Note*, he looked up the clips and saw the photos from the 1980s, the baggy uniforms, striped socks and high-tops. He read about his mom: "Another workman-like effort by senior forward Sue Patch." Susan was no star, but she was a solid starter. And in the school gymnasium, a backboard-sized team picture hangs on the wall–watching over Cooper's P.E. classes and school convocations–the most successful basketball team in school history, Sue Patch's team.

Before Cooper was big enough to heave a ball up to the rim, Susan had hung a goal on the garage. She taught Coop how to fingertip dribble, how to shoot with his elbows in, and later, how to box-out for rebounds. For years Susan has talked about how high school basketball and that season were the best things that ever happened to her. She also talks about how basketball has helped her and her brothers in their business. "People remember," she says.

Susan tells Cooper she wants him to know that special feeling of being part of the team. "I was taller and faster," Susan likes to say, "but you can make up for size and speed with desire, skills, and hustle." Often Susan urges Cooper to hone his game by playing with Kyle or his uncles. Sometimes Mom joins the two high school sophomores in a game of H–O–R–S–E. Kyle, a natural leaper, can dunk now, so they limit him to one automatic–letter–on–them slam per game.

Ready to leave, she stands at the back door, hand resting on the knob. She's told Cooper how she worked with her father and brothers and never fit in with their Old Boys Club. But things have changed. A lot more women started buying cars, SUVs, vans, and trucks, and they want to buy from a woman. That change made her number one in sales. What's more, men customers appreciate and respect her. Maybe because she played and knows basketball as well as any of them. Or maybe because she's a straight shooter about prices and add-ons.

Cooper realizes his mother said something.

"What?"

"I *said,*" she sounds irritated, "maybe you can study at school and get off work early." Then her eyebrows arch with an idea, and she snaps her fingers. "Let's get a pizza before the game."

"Maybe," Cooper says. "But I don't know, Mom."

"Forget it then," she says. "Don't be late for school," and slams the door behind her

He taps the cracked screen of his phone to check the time. He needs to leave in about ten minutes.

*

After school, Cooper enters *The Nema Note* office. Lester Bittaman, the editor, is waiting. "Hey, come here," Mr. Bittaman says. Cooper checks the clock to make sure he's not late as he eases into the indicated chair. Mr. Bittaman rises, hikes up his pants, and sits on a corner of his desk. "Dan Dorsett is sick and can't cover the Martinsville game, so I want you to do it."

"I can't," Cooper says.

"Why not?"

"I don't know how."

"Sure you do. You've read the sports page since you were a little kid, right?" Cooper half nods. "That's what you do. Take notes of important plays. Get the stats and scores. Write it up and drop it off before school tomorrow morning. Then bang," he hits the desk, "your name is in tomorrow's newspaper–your first byline."

"But–"

"Between you and me, kid," Lester Bittaman whispers, "Martinsville will probably win by 30, and nobody reads about the home team getting routed. So the pressure's off."

"*Julius Caesar!*" Cooper blurts. "I got an English test tomorrow. On *Julius Caesar*. So I can't."

Lester Bittaman calculates over his watch. "You have three hours before you have to catch the team bus–plenty of time. Study right here. I'll send somebody out to get you a sandwich."

"Team bus? I can't ride the team bus." God, the team, he thinks. After getting cut? I can't get on that bus with the guys.

"It's all arranged. And we'll pay you fifty bucks."

Fifty bucks! That's what he made for a whole day of sweeping floors and dusting showroom cars for his mother.

His mom. Cooper considers calling her, telling her about this and asking for a ride to the game. But then he thinks, no, I'll surprise her. She'll read my name in the Friday afternoon paper.

*

Before Cooper climbs aboard the team bus, Coach Davis tells the guys why Cooper is there, so he doesn't have to explain. This relieves some of the tightness across Cooper's chest but adds distance from the team. He takes a seat in the back next to a bag of towels and imagines being one of the players.

Cooper's phone pings with a text. He sees it's from Kyle Knox: "Dude, so cool you're covering the game. Good luck."

He texts back: "Good luck to you. Have a great game."

In the gym at Martinsville, Cooper sits two rows behind the team bench, one row back from the managers. He sees his mother and his Uncle Ron high in the stands behind him, on the visitors' side with a few other men. When the Sassafras County Mountaineers meander from the locker room to warm up, Cooper notices how the players scan the cavernous old 5,200-seat Martinsville gymnasium, already packed and panting a moist heat.

Then the Martinsville Artesians burst from their locker room in red, white, and blue uniforms, lifting a wave of energy from the cheering crowd, and the band strikes up the school fight song. The Sassafras County players actually stop warm-ups to watch Jerry Stokes, the six-foot four-inch Indiana All-Star, lead his team in a circle around the entire floor, staring down the Mountaineers. Then Stokes goes in for a slam dunk, and the fans go berserk. Martinsville's whole warm-up is a precision drill. Confidence emanates from them with the aplomb of champions.

Martinsville controls the tip-off, and Sassafras County falls back into a box-and-one zone defense. The tallest Mountaineer, Bob Shepherd at six-foot three, guards Jerry Stokes. But it doesn't work. Stokes dribbles full speed, then stops–Shepherd sliding past–and pulls up to sink a three-pointer. Next time, he blows by Shepherd for a lay-up. But Stokes also creates multiple-move shots. He posts up, fakes right then left, steps back as if to shoot a fall-away only to step through the double-team for a scoop shot.

Cooper, like everyone in the gym, marvels at Stokes. A few times he glances up to see his mother shake her head in admiration.

At half time, Martinsville leads by 15 points, and Sassafras County is lucky it isn't 30. Then Cooper awakes to his empty notebook. He fumbles to get out his pencil. But he can't remember any details! The first half was a blur of Stokes's dominance. Cooper checks the scorer's bench. Stokes has 18 points. Kyle Knox leads the Mountaineers with eight.

The Martinsville Artesianettes, a not–so–precision drill team in unforgiving sequined leotards, perform at halftime to an old Henry Mancini tune. Cooper watches his mother and uncle talk with other hoop zealots. Although he can't hear them, he knows how the conversation goes from their emphatic gestures and the easy nod of their heads: 'We gotta stop Stokes.'

Sassafras County wanders out to warm up for the second half in an unstructured shoot–around. Then the Artesians run from their locker room in single file again–Jerry Stokes leading his team around the floor. But this time, as they pass the Mountaineers, Kyle Knox grabs a ball and falls in along side Jerry Stokes. As they approach the basket Knox sprints ahead of Stokes and slam dunks in front of him, causing Stokes to miss his dunk.

Enraged Martinsville fans flood the gym with boos and throw programs onto the floor. Cooper looks up and notices dust sifting off the ancient rafters and falling past the lights. He sees his mother high in the stands, cheering wildly and slapping skin with her brother. While dust settles on them.

Maybe she'll never cheer for me in a basketball uniform that way, Cooper thinks, but just wait until tomorrow afternoon. All those men who stop by the dealership will say, 'Hey Susan, we saw Cooper's name in the paper. You must be proud.'

In the second half, the Mountaineers stay with a box-and-one, but now Kyle chases the older and taller Jerry Stokes and stays with him.

The first time Martinsville tries to pass to Stokes, Knox pounces for the steal. Stokes tries to cut him off, and Knox runs right over Stokes–like a blitzing linebacker crushing a quarterback. More jeering from the crowd, screaming for Kyle Knox to get thrown out, but it's a simple foul call.

Kyle practically lives in Stokes's jersey, playing deny defense. When Martinsville gets the ball to him, the All-Star can't shake Kyle. The intense defense ignites Kyle. He rips down rebounds, dives after loose balls, and hustles so hard the Martinsville fans stop booing every time he touches the ball. He develops a hot hand–the outside jumper flowing off his fingertips or muscling inside for a lay–up.

Cooper notes in the eyes of his old friend a self-confidence and thrill for the challenge. Cooper wants to feel that way about writing for the paper. Right then, he wills himself to shed his fear and seize a measure of self-confidence to meet his own challenge–he can write this story.

By the end of the third quarter, the Mountaineers close within six, but everyone knows the number–five–rated Artesians can hold off the smaller Sassafras County squad. Then in the fourth quarter, behind Knox, the Mountaineers tie the game. The lead bounces back and forth in the final minutes as the teams trade baskets.

With two seconds left, Jerry Stokes comes off a pick for an in-bounds pass and goes up for the last shot. Kyle rushes to get a hand in his face, and the three–pointer clangs off the rim. The Mountaineers win 62–60. They upset Martinsville *in* Martinsville.

The modest number of Sassafras County fans rush the floor as if they'd won the state title. Players hug each other, and cheerleaders leap into athletes' sweaty arms and kiss them. Cooper too runs onto the court. Kyle hugs him, and he slaps skin with the other players. They run off the floor together toward the locker room, Cooper right with the team.

Then, outside the locker room, Susan Patch shakes Kyle Knox's hand and hugs him. "Great game, son," she says, "great game."

Son.

Cooper hides behind others in the crowd. What the hell is Mom doing waiting outside the locker room like a groupie? he thinks. What the hell am *I* doing here? He tries to slip away, but Susan sees him. "Cooper? Hey, Cooper."

He stops but doesn't look at his mother.

"What're you doing here?" Susan asks.

"Nothing," Cooper says to the floor.

"Hey, I asked you a question."

"Covering the game."

"What?"

He looks at his mother. "Writing about it for *The Note*." Cooper moves toward the door, feeling his mother follow.

"What?" she says, "Wait," but Cooper keeps going.

In the gym, Susan catches her son by the shirtsleeve. "What's this about *writing*?"

"Mr. Bittaman gave me the assignment."

"Assignment? What assignment? I thought you had a Shakespeare test."

"The newspaper, Mom. I'm writing for the newspaper."

"Since when–" Susan frowns. "You know how to do that?"

"Well," Cooper almost lies, "not really, but I think I can do it."

"Jesus," Susan says, eyes rolling. "That was one of the biggest wins in school history. Everybody in town will want to read about how it happened. Bittaman wants *you* to tell about it? I knew you were headed for trouble when you got mixed up with that newspaper."

Cooper feels his small measure of self-confidence draining out of him, as if someone shot a hole in a bucket of water. His mother is right. The upset means everyone in the county will open the sports page first to read his story about the big upset victory. *His* story.

In that moment, Cooper wishes they had lost.

"Is this a whim, writing for a weekly newspaper?" she asks. "Have you thought about working on your game, so you can make next year's team? What would Kyle's dad be telling him to do?"

"Kyle's dad? What's–?" Cooper faces his mother, feeling a certain shame but unsure why.

Susan shakes her head at Cooper as if the answers are so obvious that her son must understand. "Maybe you should work at the dealership after school. I'm sure Chuck could use some help in the shop or in parts."

"What? I don't want to work at the dealership, Mom." He must stop this. But she's his mom. "At least not now." The small lobes of his brain scream, Why is it going in this direction? Why can't you be supportive of me? Cooper feels a heat rise in his chest but has no words.

"Mom, right now, I have a job to do. This article."

"Do you think you're too good to work at the dealership?" Susan says. "Too good for the shop?"

"No" he says, but he wants to say yes. "Why are we talking about this?" He doesn't know what's going on, doesn't know what to say. Why is she being so hard on him, so stern?

"Like it or not, Coop, that dealership is probably your future." Susan's hands open to the boy. "The sooner you recognize it, the better off you are."

Now his anger hardens into words. "You think I'm a loser because I didn't make the basketball team, Mom. Because I'm not Kyle Knox. Well, shove that."

Susan Patch's glare fails to stop her son.

"Maybe I can be better at newspaper reporting or something else than I am at basketball." Cooper pauses, letting his next thought sharpen in the silence. Then he says, "Maybe better at it than you were at basketball. And maybe better at it than you are at selling Fords."

Susan Patch doesn't answer. As the frown eases from her face, something else in her expression, something Cooper has never seen before, forms. His mother turns and strides under the basket onto the hardwood, which has ambered under generations of varnish. Cooper watches her go. Just beyond mid-court Susan pivots, "How you gettin' home?"

"I–" Cooper's voice hitches, "I got a ride on the team bus."

"Team bus, huh?" Sue's eyes sweep the stands, and her voice sounds far off. "Yeah, that's the place to be." She drifts back to Cooper. "See you at home."

On the team bus, the players talk and laugh all the way to Nema–while Cooper shares a back seat with a bag of sweaty uniforms. He tries to take notes, but there is no controlling his pencil on the bumpy secondary highway.

He thinks about what he might have said to his mother. He imagines himself saying: 'You think basketball is important. Our stupid town thinks basketball is important. Maybe I don't. Maybe it isn't, and neither is your stupid pint–sized dealership.' But he knows he can't say it.

At school, everyone goes in to get books and drop off equipment. Cooper grabs a clipboard with pages of statistics for scoring, assists, steals, and rebounds. Kyle held Jerry Stokes to six points in the second half, 24 for the night, while scoring 26 himself and leading the team with 12 rebounds. As he copies the numbers and takes a photo of the stat sheet with his phone to be sure he got it right, Coop hears players joking in the hall as they leave. The heavy doors by the gym slam with an echo in the empty hall.

After the last players leave, Cooper finishes copying the stats and begins walking home. The cold night opens to a star-filled sky, but his mind clouds with scores, and fouls, and rebounds. Cooper writes the beginning of the article in his head as he walks. That sounds good, he thinks. To remember, he tries to recite it, but the pieces don't mesh. He starts to run, thinking if he gets home he can write it down. But when Cooper rushes to the kitchen table with pencil and paper, the words vanish.

He hears the TV in the living room. Susan, on the couch, waits for the sports on the 11:00 news to see the scores. Nobody knows more about basketball than his mom, maybe she'll help Cooper get started.

"Hey, Mom."

"Hey, Coop," Susan's eyes don't leave the commercial for Di-Giorno frozen pizza. "Bet the guys were pretty excited on the team bus."

"Yeah." Cooper stays at the door. They both watch TV, the weather starts, continued cold with snow likely over the weekend. "Hey, Mom," Cooper hedges, "think you could help me with this article?"

Her eyes stay on the television, but Cooper notices her jaw muscles flex.

"Mom?"

"I heard you," she says and turns. "What do you want?"

"Can you help me remember some important plays? Maybe help me get started?"

Susan mutes the TV and turns to Cooper. She talks about Kyle dunking ahead of Stokes before the second half and how his knocking Stokes to the floor changed the game's momentum. She mentions a few key scores, a steal, a rebound, a tip-in. Cooper takes notes. Suddenly, Susan stops and turns back to the television.

"How do you think I should start, Mom?"

"What are you asking me for? Look—" She purses up her lips in thought. "You know what I think? I think you should call the editor and tell him to forget it." Susan rocks forward in her chair. "He's got no business asking you to do this."

"It's too late to call. It's due in the morning. And it's my job."

His Mother gets up and shuts off the TV as soon as the sports gives a brief on the upset victory, and goes to the stairs. "This could be one of those hard lessons. Don't take on a job you can't do. You got yourself into this mess. You get yourself out."

Screw you, Cooper lashes out in his head. You stink. I give up my weekends to help you at the crappy little dealership, but you won't give me fifteen minutes when I need it. Thanks a lot.

Back at the kitchen table, he tries to forget his mother and concentrate on the game. It is 11:30. Just put something down, Cooper orders himself, like you see in the sports page, anything. "Kyle Knox shines in big victory," he writes at the top. "Kyle Knox led the Mountaineers to victory over number-five-rated Martinsville." He pauses. Recalling the confidence he saw in Kyle's eye, he pushes his pencil on, scratching out how Kyle's running ahead to dunk before Jerry Stokes set the tone for the second half's one-on-one match-up and the come-from-behind victory. Cooper struggles along, searching for words, and forcing out details.

Then, as if by some magic, the game's key plays reveal themselves, one suggesting another. He can hardly write it down fast enough. He doesn't know where the words come from, or if they're right. He just hopes the stream doesn't dry up. It flows out of him as naturally as the ball rotated off Kyle Knox's fingers. Swish. But it can't be that good, he thinks.

He doesn't know how to end, so he ends it as the night did, with the "happy babble of high school athletes that continued until the last player left Sassafras County High School with the echoing slam of the heavy doors by the gymnasium." Leaving behind the statistics and the pride of a major victory.

The next morning, Cooper is downstairs at the kitchen table before daylight, working his article over in ink. When he hears his mother's footsteps coming downstairs, he calls, "Hey Mom, can you listen to this? It's my article about last night's game. Tell me what you think."

Susan lifts her coat off the back door hook and freezes. Then she says, "Wish I could Coop, but I have to get to work early."

"If Knox wrote it," Cooper mumbles, "you'd listen."

"What?" Susan snaps.

The corners of Cooper's mouth stiffen. He wants to scream at his mother, but Susan goes out the back door, leaving her thermos on the counter. Gone before Cooper can say anything, even if he knew what to say.

*

Friday morning when Cooper walks into *The Note* before school, Lester Bittaman's look registers surprise at seeing him. Mr. Bittaman takes the pages, full of Cooper's observations and careful penmanship.

"Why didn't you email it to me. Why isn't this typed?"

"We don't have a computer at home. When I need one, I use one at school, the library, or at my mom's office. All of them were closed last night." Cooper feels a little ashamed. "And you didn't say it had to be typed."

"I shouldn't have to. We don't have time to decipher this chicken scratch."

"I could type it up during study hall," Cooper said, "and email it to you."

A heavy sigh pours from Bittaman's nose as he glances over the first page. He shakes his head. "You lead with second-half warm-ups? What were you thinking?"

Cooper can't answer, his eyes lock on the editor's penny loafers. He's never owned a pair of loafers.

"There's no time for you to type it and email it. I'll have to get someone to rewrite it. You got the stats, I see. At least we can get a box score out of it."

You have to read it, Cooper wants to demand. I worked too hard for you not to read it. But the words won't come out.

"You didn't even put your name on it, for crying out loud. What's your name again?"

"Patch," his voice cracks, "Cooper Patch."

"Well, Mr. Patch," Lester Bittaman says as he writes Cooper's name on the paper, "I suggest you get your hands on a computer, and learn what a lead is if you want to be a reporter."

After a pause, Bittaman again sighs, and his voice softens. "Next time you'll know."

There won't be a next time, Cooper understands. He'll have to work at the dealership. But he says nothing. He leaves. You shoulda known better than to try, he tells himself—it's trash anyway. There's your lesson.

That afternoon, when the final bell rings, Cooper doesn't want to face the editor. But he has to go to work. He didn't quit his job as a copy boy, and he wasn't fired, was he? Besides, even facing Bittaman is easier than going home.

When he walks into the newsroom, Lester Bittaman sees him. "There he is: Cooper Patch, cub reporter." And Mr. Bittaman holds up *The Nema Note*. "SASSAFRAS COUNTY 'KNOX' OFF MARTINSVILLE 62-60," it says, right on the front page, and below: "Special Report by High School Correspondent, Cooper Patch."

Bittaman laughs at Cooper's shocked face. "I told Bill to rewrite your story, and he told me to reconsider. It was terrific the way you captured that half-time dunk and how it motivated the team for the second-half comeback. That takes more than a knowledge of basketball, it takes a talent—or luck." He waves his finger at Cooper: "You might have a knack for newswriting, kid."

"Thanks," Cooper mumbles.

"And here. This is yours," he hands Cooper a check for 50 dollars. "The first of many. Okay?"

His eyes focus on the check. "Sure, Mr. Bittaman."

"Welcome to the team," the editor says. "And when you go home, you see that laptop on the desk over there?" Cooper looks. "Take that with you. It's old, but it works."

"Yessir."

The Note employees are gathered, and when Lester Bittaman finishes, they shake Cooper's hand and pat him on the back.

"You got the scoop, Coop."

"Good work, kid."

"Welcome to the team."

After work, Cooper hoists the laptop and puts it in his back-
pack. He likes the weight of it. With the check in his wallet, five
copies of *The Nema Note* under his arm, and the laptop, Cooper Patch
forgets the pain of the previous night and the shame he carried all
day. He remembers only the sweet stream of words and voices of
congratulation.

When Susan Patch gets home late, Cooper hustles into the
kitchen where he placed a copy of the paper on the table. He
hopes for praise but expects less. Shielded by the support of the
newspaper staff and several congratulatory text messages and a
couple of phone calls from classmates, including one from Kyle, he
can withstand a cutting word from his mother. Over the last few
hours he has rehearsed a series of comebacks.

"Hi, Mom." Instantly he recognizes in the hint of slack posture
that his mother has been drinking. It doesn't happen often, usually
when something sets her off.

"Hey, Coop." her eyes settle on *The Note*. "I heard about this,"
she says. A hand with no rings lifts the paper off the Formica and
drops it back down. "With that kind of effort, you'll make next
year's team."

"I ain't gonna try out," Cooper states.

"That right?"

"That's right. I'm through with basketball, Mom." A tightness
swells across Cooper's chest and back, readying for a fight–a physical one if need be–as he waits for his mother's response.

Susan is gazing down at the table, still wearing her coat, no
doubt collecting her thoughts for a cutting remark, and then a de-
parture to let Cooper stew in it.

Cooper waits.

She slings her purse on the kitchen counter.

"You ought to have quote marks right there," his mother finally says, pointing to a sentence near the bottom of the first column. "I gave you those words, 'The emotional turning point was confirmed when Kyle Knox knocked Jerry Stokes to the floor during an attempted steal early in the second half.'"

"I wrote that. You can't take no cred–"

A hand rises like a casual traffic cop, a hand with creases of age, and it stops the boy. The mother lifts but an eye, "I'm readin'"

They stand there a long time–the mother bending her neck over the paper on the table and flipping to the sports page to finish the article. The boy fixes on the side of his mother's head and remains braced, self-consciously assuming a fighter's stance.

Finally, Susan closes the paper. She takes off her coat and hangs it by the back door. Back at the paper, her finger taps that sentence. "You were smart enough to take a line or two from me and put them in the right place. I'm no literature scholar or newspaper reporter, but that reads pretty damn good to me, son."

Son.

"Thanks, Mom." He speaks softly but remains guarded.

"I didn't know you had such a good handle on the sport."

"Had a good teacher, all those games you been dragging me to since I could walk."

Susan smiles, nods. Her focus is on the newspaper again, "Yeah, I 'spose I taught you more 'bout basketball than you ever wanted or needed to know." She shakes her head at herself, "Spent a lot of time trying to figure out how to help a boy become a man."

"Sure helped last night."

"I suppose." She pauses. "But you know," she glances up at him and back down, rubbing her forehead, smoothing eyebrows, "I couldn't have done this. I didn't think you could do it either. You surprised me. You had the guts to try, and you succeeded. I'm proud of you." She paused. "Not so proud of myself, I have to admit."

This is the sadness that caused her to drink, Cooper thinks, and he wants to lift it. "Beginner's luck," the boy says and laughs.

Susan slaps the counter—angry eyes lock on Cooper. "Don't you pull that. You *did* something here. Now you claim it. You found out you might be good at something, might have a special talent. Take pride in it. Build on it. Never sell yourself short like I sold you short last night." She snatches up the paper and shakes it at him. "This was a bigger win for you than it was for the boys on that damn basketball team."

They are quiet for a long time. Susan sits at the table, and after a bit Cooper hops up to sit on the kitchen counter, heels dangling against the lower cabinet. In the quiet that stretches on and on, Cooper mulls it over and knows his mother is right.

At last he breaks the silence: "Mr. Bittaman paid me 50 dollars and gave me a laptop to write my future stories."

"Then you're buying the pizza," Susan says.

"Is that your fee for working as my hoop analyst?"

"Damn straight."

Fire in the Field

It was a hot day, the day I burned the field. Chores filled the morning, and I hurried because Mom said when I finished I could ride my bike the three miles to see my friends in the nearby suburb. One of the last chores was to burn the trash, and I lugged the barrel to the fire circle at the edge of my grandfather's field.

The field, which surrounded our yard, stood in hay that year, drying in the relentless August sun, about due for a final cutting and baling. Within a minute of my lighting the fire, the wind picked up, lifting a piece of flaming paper out of the fire ring into the field. I ran to stomp out the small fire, but when I turned, three or four more pieces took flight, blowing past me to scatter in the field.

Like an unleashed pack of foxhounds, the fire rushed into the dry hay. I ran to the garage and grabbed an old blanket to put it out before anyone saw, but by the time I got back, it was out of control. Flames raced across the grass, as the sound of fire rose from a faint whoosh to a loud rushing and crackling like something alive, pumping heat and smoke into the hot air. Oh no, everyone would see. Everyone would know of my giant mistake. I sprinted back to the garage where my old man was pounding wrinkles out of a fender—and told him.

He ran out of the garage. "Goddamnit!" he yelled. He snatched up my t-shirt. "You're gonna pay for this." He shucked me aside and ran back to the garage. He snapped off a broom handle over his thigh, then snapped it again, cursing me under his breath. At first I thought he'd club me with the broken handle, but instead he tore rags and made slapdash torches and splashed kerosene over them. His hand shoved me. "Grab some blankets and get them wet!"

We had a stack of wool army blankets. I grabbed two and ran to the hose.

What had I done? How could I have done this?

He was yelling at me, and I ran with the heavy, dripping blankets. He waited in his pickup truck, engine revving. I started to go to the door but thought better and jumped in the back with the wet blankets. The truck fishtailed through the gravel and across the yard and then bounced into the field. I struggled to keep my feet and squatted, pressing myself into a corner of the truck bed. He took a sharp turn, racing around the fire, and I almost fell out.

Was he trying to toss me out?

Would he shove me into the fire?

It was what I deserved. How did I do this? You can't fix this, I thought.

He slammed to a stop at the far end of the field. I grabbed a cold, wet blanket and jumped out. He snapped open his lighter and held up the torches with their crude petroleum smell. I knew what to do—he'd told me before: fight fire with fire, one of the oldest rules in the book. We sprinted into the hay ahead of the flames, choking on the smoke, tears flowing from my eyes, and we started back-fires with our torches. I started for the woods to keep the fire from the trees, from the birds and animals.

"NO! Save the corn first, you idiot!" my father screamed. I was an idiot. How stupid can you be, Jason?

The corn, an 80-acre field, and nothing protected it but an old wire fence, a man, an eleven-year-old idiot, two blankets and two lousy torches.

I looked up. Flames tall as a horse now galloped toward us. Smoke and heat blowing, rolling ahead on the wind. I sprinted ahead to protect the corn.

The hastily made torches allowed flaming kerosene to run down over my hands, burning me and leaving a burned-hair smell on my forearms, but the pain wasn't bad enough to pause for. Besides, this was no time to make a fuss. Once we got the backfires going, we had to control them against the wind with the wet blankets—to keep them from spreading into the fence row and the dry cornfield behind us. I still worried about the woods, the birds and animals. We threw the wet blankets down, stomping the fire out, then threw them on the next patch of flames. We worked as fast as we could, a few feet at a time.

Dad stayed at the east end of the field to watch the downwind backfire. I was on the run again, starting backfires to protect the woods. Behind these fires was a blackened waste, a ruined twelve-acre hayfield, but I didn't pause to look at it. There was more fire to put out. I choked on the smoke but ran hard anyway.

As I ran to save the woods I loved, the woods I'd put at risk, I thought of the first time I was in this field. It was six years ago. I was five. My grandparents had offered my mother and father an acre to build a house. It followed a reconciliation between my father and his parents.

It was a beautiful spring day, endless blue skies. Nothing like the day of the fire. The field had been plowed and disked, ready for planting. Mom led the way. My older brother, my father, and I followed. She took her time. At several points, she stopped and turned slowly, holding out her arms as if framing the view.

"April," Dad said, "come on, let's just pick a spot."

She ignored him and continued her survey, tromping through the dusty field.

"April–"

She spun on her heel, hands on her hips: "Walt, this is where we'll raise Walter and Jason. I will walk this field and choose the spot for our home. If I want to walk it five times, then I'll walk it five times."

Dad stood nearly a foot taller than Mom and was twice her weight, but she stared him down. I was afraid it might get ugly. But it didn't this time.

He smiled and held his hands up as if to stop a bus, "Okay, Ape. Okay. Take your time, you're right."

"Darn right, I'm right," she said in a lighthearted way and gave my brother a playful shove, which made us boys laugh. Then April Blake went on about her business, and we followed her. She picked a spot at the opposite corner of the field from the white, Indiana farmhouse where Dad had grown up.

Just before Christmas, we moved into our simple new ranch house at the corner of 86th Street and Mud Creek Road. After our string of cramped rentals, it felt like a mansion carved out of a corn field.

But this year, the field was in hay–and the hay was on fire. And the cornfield next to it was in danger.

Fire rolled toward the woods. I had to stop it.

I sprinted ahead of the closest flames, the hottest flames. My lungs forced a cough in the smoke, and I put the flaming torch to the hay, starting the backfire. Once that section was controlled, I started the next spot, and the next.

On and on I worked without looking for my father. It was hard to see, my throat and eyes burned. I was parched, my hands now bleeding after the blisters burst, but I dared not complain or ask for water. It was a long afternoon. Eventually, Dad brought me a shovel to help bury the remaining fire. He threw it on the ground at my feet.

He growled, "Damnit, son, sometimes you're more trouble than you're worth," and he spit to the side.

"I'm going in for supper," he said. "You finish what you started." And he left me to work alone. His words replayed over and over in my head as I chased down final flames and shoveled smoldering areas of the field and pounded out embers.

When Walter got home from his summer job as a house painter, he brought me water and helped me. My seventeen-year-old brother tried to joke with me about it.

"Jason, I didn't know you hated baling hay this much."

But I couldn't laugh it off, not the loss of twelve acres of hay. My brother went inside to eat. I made another check, walking the perimeter of the field with the shovel and a wet blanket, shoveling out and stomping on smoldering clumps.

From the hedge, my mother called me for supper, but I waved her off. I couldn't believe the trouble I'd caused. What would my grandparents think? What would they do? I couldn't quit until every flicker of fire was out. It was dusk before I finished.

I sat on the pile of rocks at the top of a small hill in the field, surrounded by charred earth, still smoking and smoldering in places. The sky going purple promised to hide what I'd done, at least until dawn. My hands were burned and bloodied, the hair on my arms singed off, bloody blisters forming on my forearms, too. The rubber soles of my workboots had melted, and my lungs hurt from breathing smoke for seven hours. I was fall-down exhausted. But I couldn't go inside and face my parents. Especially my father.

"Jason," my mother's voice close and soft at my shoulder surprised me. I hadn't heard her coming across the field. "Come on inside now."

I couldn't speak to her or look at her. I felt so ashamed and stupid for the fire and for having complained about chores earlier in the day. "I got to make sure it's all out."

"You put it out," she said.

I still hadn't looked at her. I couldn't. How could I tell Mom I was afraid to face my father, afraid to be in the same house? I felt embarrassed beyond words. What kind of person caused such destruction? Not Walter, that's for sure. I was just a dumb eleven-year-old boy. A stupid kid. More trouble than I was worth.

We stood silently in the blackened field for a bit, my head down. Smoke smoldered nearby. Then I felt Mom's hand rub my back, then up to the back of my neck and across my shoulders. I swallowed down the knot in my throat. I wanted to fall down on my knees and bury my face against her skirt, but I was too old for that.

"It was an accident," she said. "Could've happened to anybody."

"But it happened to me," I choked out, unable to imagine it happening to my older brother, the star athlete about to start his senior year of high school. Walter had burned plenty of trash in the same fire ring without a problem.

"Oh, Honey, it was an accident. It's okay. Nobody got hurt. Nobody's going to say anything about it. Nobody's mad at you."

I found this hard to believe. Besides, I was angry with myself. "Come on inside now and get cleaned up and have some dinner."

"I got to check a few more spots."

"Okay, but you come in soon."

I nodded. "Okay," I whispered.

She went back to the house, and I went to the far end of the field alone with my shovel. I zig-zagged around, turning over and stomping out any last smoldering clumps.

When I came back into the house, Dad was sitting in his Lazy

Boy, the television on while he read the paper. He didn't acknowledge me. But he never mentioned the fire again, and neither did
my grandparents.

I lay in bed that night exhausted, my arms sore and sticky with
antiseptic Mom had applied, and I wore a long-sleeved t-shirt like
a bandage over my arms. I couldn't sleep. My lungs and eyes hurt.
Walter slept in the other bed. The fan hummed in the window,
blowing warm air over us, that and the smell of the charred field.

*

Something happened in the burned field. Almost immediately,
small green sprouts sprang above the black. Millions of them in
bright green. More and taller every day. It was beautiful. A little
rain, and the field sprang to life. I had done something terrible,
but in one week, it turned into something beautiful. At dusk, deer
drifted into the field and rabbits materialized around the edges to
eat the soft, lush shoots.

I stood at the edge of the field on Friday night and thought for
the first time how resilient nature was. The earth was made for life.

In a Delicate Condition

We learned of Dixon's cancer a month ago. Now he sleeps constantly, twelve or fourteen hours a day. Meanwhile, I lie awake next to him, feeling my twenty-eight-year-old husband dying. I try to read, comprehending nothing but turning the pages nonetheless, and I notice when the clock flicks from 1:43 in the morning to 1:44, thinking he's a little farther gone. Then an unsteady quiver runs through my bowels. I grip Dixon's shoulder as if to stabilize myself and pull him back.

My touch doesn't wake him.

Dixon's long stretches of deep sleep have become like a practice for being dead. When the alarm goes off, I have to shake him awake, thinking one morning I'll do this and he'll never wake up.

And I can't keep the panic from rising in my voice as I shake him, "Dixon. Dixon? Wake up Dixon!"

To save money to build our log house, we live in his uncle's tin can of a camper trailer parked on our land. That Airstream would be pure comfort on the road, I'm sure, but for daily living, it makes my folks' double-wide look like paradise. The plan was to live in the camper for about a year, until the house was finished. The exterior is almost done, stacked up like giant Lincoln Logs. Then we'd wanted to start a family in a few years. But there are no years now. The doctor gives Dixon eight to ten months. This doesn't sink in easily. I mean, *old* people die of cancer. I'm twenty-four and Dixon is twenty-eight—we don't think in months. We live right now, or years into the future. The only thing we can relate to is the school year. Since we found out in September, Dixon has until the end of the school year to live—the rest of his life, about the length of eighth grade.

We've stayed buttoned up about the cancer. But it weighs plenty on our minds and we will have to tell his family soon. Living in a space as small as this 28-foot Airstream, I can sense a budding idea before he says anything. But I didn't expect what he said after breakfast this morning, "Jan, I think we should have a baby." I was doing the dishes in the tiny sink when he said it, and it hit my ear like one of my daddy's drunken slaps. I still haven't grasped the reality that my husband will die by spring or early summer, and now he wants to have a baby?

Before I could come out of my stunned state, he told a story about his father taking him fishing to a special spot in Pepper Creek. His father, the whole Pesby family, really—mother, two sisters, and a brother—are wonderful people. If I didn't love Dixon, and I do, I would marry him just to be part of the Pesby family and escape my own. But I don't want to go into the details of my family. I know I'm lucky to have Dixon and his family.

Anyway, Dixon explained that when his daddy took him fishing that time–Dixon was in second grade–his father had said, "If you ever hear the duck-and-cover horn, I want you to know I'm coming for you. I may not get there, but I want you to know that I'm running in your direction as fast as I can. I'll be coming for you and your sisters and your brother. Okay?" Little Dixon nodded even though he'd never heard of a duck-and-cover horn. Schools had stopped doing air-raid drills before Dixon started first grade (the thought of Russia bombing the little town of Nema, Indiana seems as likely as Kentucky attacking from across the river). But his father's voice had been so serious and his eyes had welled up as he spoke, so Dixon was afraid to ask about the horn. For the next few years, every time the school had a fire drill, Dixon looked around, half-expecting to see his father sprinting across the school yard.

After his story, Dixon tips his Chicago Cubs baseball cap back on his head and waits for me to answer about a baby. Simple as that. As if it's a decision about white or bone colored toilets and bathroom sinks, as if his story makes it all clear why we should have children.

Well, it wasn't clear to me at all. "You want to try to have children," I said, "with you sick and all?" By the doctor's estimate, he will die before I could give birth. "It's crazy, Dixon. You can't ask me to do that. I'd be all alone with a baby, and how would I manage?"

He looked at the floor and picked his teeth. "Just think about it will you?" he said. "I never asked much of you. And I know I'm asking too much now. I know it's selfish. I know it'll be hard for you, but my family will help. All's I ever wanted was to marry you, and build a log house in the woods, and have a family. I know it ain't fair to ask. Almost as unfair as me getting bone cancer."

I sat on the bench in the Airstream's kitchenette, the one that folds down into another bed (sleeps six!) and dried my hands on the dishtowel. I kept rubbing: I rubbed the towel over them until the friction burned. He couldn't wait any longer for my answer and left for work, kissing me with dry, cool lips.

On my way to work at the IGA, I stopped to see Dr. Foster. The doctor was busy, so they had me talk to his nurse, Donna. I asked her what I should do and how to give Dixon some fulfillment other than getting pregnant. Donna told me it was best to plug along as normally as possible, Dixon punching-in at Westinghouse for the paycheck. She suggested I find a hobby, something Dixon and I could do together as things got worse.

So, instead of buying two tickets for an around-the-world cruise, I went to the post office and blew $85 on a Stamp Collector's Starter Set.

When Dixon walked in tonight, I–pumped up with phony enthusiasm–presented the stamps as if they were a great discovery. Stamp collecting is America's most popular hobby I tell him. If millions of people love stamps, surely we can. But Dixon shows no interest.

We don't talk much over dinner and dinners are short these days. I wrap plastic around the left-over pork chops and mashed potatoes. The small, harvest-gold refrigerator is packed with left-overs slowly going bad under plastic. I haven't adjusted to Dixon's loss of appetite, and I want him to have a nice, hot meal every night.

After clearing the table, I sit down to look over the stamps. Dixon mentions having a baby again, and I don't look up from the stamp collection right away. I've lined them up on the table, thinking if I shuffle them enough I'll get interested in them (and hope Dixon will). After all, America's most popular hobby!

When I look up, Dixon's blue-gray eyes are waiting. He wears his Cubs baseball cap, a red chamois shirt, and jeans. I don't know what to say. I tilt my head to one side, offer a tight-lipped smile, and hook my hair behind my ear. Looking up I see in the overhead light fixture, exposed in the harsh glare like an x-ray, the shadow of a dead fly. I want to clean, to snatch up the vacuum or whip out a dust rag. Watch me make that tin can sparkle, order, polish—control can be had with a little elbow grease.

"I really want to have a baby, Jan," he says.

I glance at my stamps, and it dawns on me that I can rearrange them by color. I hold up an Abraham Lincoln. "Where was this president raised?" Dixon doesn't answer. "From the age of seven to twenty-one, Honest Abe was a Hoosier boy, like you, Dixon." I grin like an idiot, but he doesn't return my smile. I feel like a nincompoop for such a featherbrained diversion.

He holds up his hand to stop my blithering and asks, "Does that mean no?"

"There's so much going on, Dixon. You're sick. And the house is being built." I pause. "If you said, 'Let's buy a sports car,' I'd say, 'Go for it.'"

"I don't want a sports car."

"You want a baby."

"And you don't?"

"I didn't say that."

We are quiet. My thoughts swirl as I regroup my stamps by color: a baby, having a baby, a little boy, a little girl, being pregnant. I haven't planned for this—Dixon's death *or* a child. I'm not ready. I want him to enjoy his last months. I want to stop everything, so I can catch up, so I can take it slow, so I can pay attention to what's left, and understand it all and get ready. But Dixon is talking again.

"Look, I know it will be hard as a single mother, especially on a cashier's pay." He takes off his hat and scratches his head, and I imagine his light-brown hair already thinning from the chemo. "And I know it's not fair or reasonable to ask you."

That's right, that's right, I think.

"When Grandpa died a few years ago," he says, "I figured Mom, and the aunts and uncles, and all us grandkids were only alive 'cause he was, so Grandpa could never really die." Dixon tips his cap back on his head and the overhead light makes his face look waxen. "So it's like–" his voice thins to a whisper, "–like there'd be nothing of me to go on."

I feel as hollow as the cheap doors of the Airstream, but I am afraid to reach very far to him. "Your log house is almost finished," I say. "That's your creation, a part of you that will go on."

His eyes register a disappointment that shames me for having said that. The supper dishes need to be washed, and I want to get started.

"I love you," I say.

"Then have my baby," he shoots back. At that he rocks out of the La-Z-Boy and leaves. The door slam shakes the length of the Airstream.

I pull back the vinyl curtains to watch Dixon, in the cool October evening, climb the hill to check the progress and work on our log house. He crosses through ribbons of shadow and light as the day's last sunshine snaps between the tree trunks.

Since Dixon worked as a carpenter before going on the line at Westinghouse, he planned to finish the interior of the house himself–with help from his brother and father. As soon as we found out about his cancer, we tried to borrow enough to hire a crew to finish the house, but the bank refused because Dixon has no life insurance.

Leaving the bank that day, I took his hand and he weakly returned my grip. I feared he might never live in his house, and I wondered how I'd get by when he was gone. Thinking about having a baby, that question roars back. How would I get by?

A husband, a house, a family–all my plans slipping through my fingers. No Cub Scout Den Mother, or Campfire Girls Leader. No Christmas mornings by the fire in our log house before going to the Pesby family Christmas dinners. And suddenly the question is, should I try, like Dixon, to grab all the dreams in a matter of months, or should I let them go and start over? I'm a young woman and, although not beautiful or pretty in the *Glamour Magazine* way,

I am not unattractive.

Having a baby would scare off single men. Who asked out a pregnant woman? Or one with an infant on her hip? I could just see it: You want my phone number? Sure, just hold my baby for a second, and I'll write it down. Is back of a Pampers okay?

*

I find myself looking down a lot these days. My chin literally resting on my chest, as if I'm praying or deep in thought, but I have no thoughts or prayers. Or perhaps I look like a third-grader admiring brand-new shoes. When I catch myself looking down, I lift my head to the trees or clouds or ceiling only to discover myself later looking at the floor again, and I wonder how long I've gone on like that. At work last week, Bobby, the high school bag-boy, bent close to the floor and asked, "What'd you lose, Jan?"

"Nothing," I answered, wishing it were true.

From the small window over the camper-sink, I watch for Dixon to return while I wash dishes. The warm water makes the fingertips of my right hand throb.

At work, when a customer approaches, I snap out of my down-cast stupor and throw myself into ringing up the sale, determined to be the best cashier in the whole IGA chain. I pound the keys so hard I bruise my fingertips.

"Honey?" a customer this afternoon said.

I looked up. It was Grandma Pesby, who I loved like my own grandmother, actually far more than my own grandmother.

"Grandma, hi," I said, bending across the conveyor belt to kiss her cheek.

Her eyes held me. "You got something against that register, Jan?"

"Oh, no, Grandma," I said, "just working hard."

She took my hand in hers, turned it over and massaged my fingertips. "What's wrong, Jan?"

But I couldn't tell her. Dixon and I haven't told anyone yet. We have to soon, but how do you tell a family like his that the youngest son is dying at age twenty–eight? If I have his child, I'll be part of the loving Pesby family forever, and if I don't, that relationship will slowly evaporate after Dixon's death. A rapid loss of the man I love, and a slow, crushing loss of his loving clan.

The western sky has turned the color of copper by the time I finish the dishes and Dixon still isn't back. I lift my jacket off the hook by the door. As I put it on, I see my stamps and realize the faces are those of dead men. I sweep them up and jam them in my pocket. I go out and up the hill to find Dixon. He wants me to have a baby, I think as I climb. Why can't this be a decision like so many we made on the house? We settled for cheap doors, faucets, and light fixtures with the plan to buy good ones later. This baby decision is black or white, no room for grays. I like grays–we all like grays.

If I do it, I'll probably be six or eight months pregnant when he dies. I'll be alone when I go into labor on a hot and muggy July or August night. As a single parent I'll have to juggle work and child rearing. Tight money. It's all too much for me. Way too much. Dixon, I want to cry out, how can you ask me to do this? I can't do this alone.

A 'no' will hang an overcast through our last six or eight months, a gloomy wait for death. The fights will be short–slashing deeply with a few cruel words. Leaving wounds without the time to heal. I don't think we can survive that much pressure packed into a 28-foot Airstream. I picture Dixon, a strong man gone weak in his last days: his fogged-over eyes accusing me of letting him die. I can't face that.

I reach the house and go inside. Hard to see in the dark, I stumble over building materials. "Dixon?" I half-whisper, climbing the roughed-out stairs, "Dixon, where are you?" Then I hear the whine of a chain saw and pass through the studded skeleton of a wall and inch to the dormer of the second bedroom. The unfinished window opens to the evening air which carries the sound of the saw up and over me so I can feel its vibration in my breasts and smell the oil in the jet of blue exhaust.

Below me, on the downward slope, Dixon circles a dead beech tree. I put my hand in my pocket and feel the stamps. Those stupid stamps with the faces of dead men. He revs the saw and drives the blade into the gray trunk, cutting so the tree will fall downhill. A shower of sawdust from the dead tree gushes over his hips and legs. There are two things we can do together now, and his brother and father will see to it that our house gets finished. Slowly the old beech tree tips, and Dixon backs into the undergrowth.

When the beech falls, the view opens, and I see in the day's last light the hills of southern Indiana swelling out of a blue haze across the horizon. I realize the choice is black or white, life or death. I have to live with either bad choice, but Dixon can only live with one. The decision flies like an arrow through the window and across the room, sticking in the log wall. I toss those pointless stamps out the window, and I call to him.

"Hey, you," I sing down after Dixon shuts off the saw.

"Hey, yourself." He smiles. "How's the view from there now?"

I look out at the lovely, timeless hills, appreciated by who knows how many generations in the past and how many more in the future, and I think, Okay, Jan if this is the decision, live it all the way for him and for yourself and for the baby. Even as the words come out of my mouth—"I think our child will love it"—I'm thinking oh, Jan, what'd you just get yourself into?